In memory of Rose

Piggy Monk Square

Grace Jolliffe

LARGE PRINT

Oxford

First published in Great Britain 2005
by
Tindal Street Press Ltd.

Published in Large Print 2006 by ISIS Publishing Ltd.,
7 Centremead, Osney Mead, Oxford OX2 0ES
by arrangement with
Tindal Street Press Ltd.

British Library Cataloguing in Publication Data
Jolliffe, Grace
    Piggy Monk Square. – Large print ed.
    1. Squatters – Fiction
    2. Liverpool (England) – Fiction
    3. Suspense fiction
    4. Large type books
    I. Title
    823.9'2 [F]

ISBN 0–7531–7573–8 (hb)
ISBN 0–7531–7574–6 (pb)

Printed and bound in Great Britain by
T. J. International Ltd., Padstow, Cornwall

Acknowledgements

Special thanks to: Emma Hargrave and Alan Mahar at Tindal Street Press for their warmth, wisdom and patience; my family for their encouragement; and my friends James and Maria for their never-ending support.

ACKNOWLEDGMENTS

CHAPTER
ONE

My name's Rebecca but me mates call me Sparra cos of me legs. I live in the best street in Liverpool. Mind you, even though it's the best street there's still not much to do. The old ladies go mad if we play ball in case we break the windows, so we can either play skip or we can sit on the step and watch who's coming up and down.

Loads of people come down our street cos we've got Mister Abdul's shop in the middle and that's where everyone gets their messages. Mister Abdul's always smiling and he knows everybody's names. He's dead brainy cos he knows what everyone wants to buy, even before they tell him. The other day I went in and he said, "Ah little Rebecca, let me see, you want a medium sliced and a flying saucer if there's a penny over." He was right too. There was only one day when he got it wrong cos he said, "Ah little Rebecca, let me see, you want a medium sliced and a packet of tea and a red liquorice if there's a penny over." Well I did want the red liquorice but me Mam only wanted the medium sliced and Mister Abdul didn't smile when I told him, then, the minute I got home, me Mam said, "Oh Rebecca I forgot to tell you to get tea, you'll have to run

1

back." I was back in two seconds and Mister Abdul laughed his head off and gave me a purple torpedo for free.

My best mate, Debbie, says Mister Abdul's got special eyes that can see into everyone's cupboard and everyone's got those kind of eyes where he comes from, so that's why they always have shops. I didn't believe her so we went in and asked him one day. He just laughed, wiggled his eyes around, and said a good shopkeeper couldn't tell his secrets to two little girls even if they were the prettiest in the street.

I don't think he was right about that though. I'm not pretty, not like me Mam, she's got lovely shiny hair and mine's all knotty. I'm not pretty like Debbie either, cos she's got long red hair and she always wears a red spotty mac. She's got a long thin neck, nearly as thin as me legs, so she looks a bit like a bottle of ketchup. I love ketchup and sometimes, if me tea's not ready, I sit on the step and eat a ketchup buttie and that's what I'm doing now, cos now's the time the bad men come driving their cars along our street and we all have to watch out for them.

They always come down at teatime. Sometimes they slow down beside us, call us over and try to give us money. They wear stripey suits and spotty ties and they all have short grey hair and lots of wrinkles. Sometimes they're really fat and sometimes they're really thin, but thin or fat they always wear suits and ties.

Me Mam told me all about them, they've got loads of money but it's not real money. It's only pretend money and it's poisoned! If you even touch it you're dead. Debbie says they don't really want to poison us. What they really want to do is take us away in their cars and fiddle with us. Me Mam says not to take any notice of Debbie cos she's got an old head. I don't know what that means cos Debbie's only nine like me. Anyway, she's me bezzie mate and I have to take notice of her, don't I?

We don't want to get fiddled with or poisoned so if we're walking down the street and we see one we always run away, except when I'm with me Mam. Sometimes when we go to the shops they follow us and sometimes they shout, "How much?"

Mam always tells them to go and get lost. She says if she had a gun she'd shoot the whole lot of them. I'm glad she hasn't got a gun cos she'd probably have to go to jail for ever and ever amen, cos she'd have to shoot hundreds and millions of them if she wanted to shoot them all.

Bad men don't always have cars though, me Dad told me that. He says there's another kind, the kind that put kids in old sacks, tie the top so they can't get out, then throw them in the Mersey. Me Dad says we should never go down the entries behind our houses cos they could be hiding there and we should never go to the park on our own cos that's where they live. One time when I went to the park with me Dad, one of them came out of the bushes. He had the dirtiest face I'd ever seen and there was dribble on his chin. He was wearing lots of jumpers and a scruffy old coat. He was carrying an old empty sack. He came up to me Dad and asked him for spare coppers but me Dad said he had no change and Dirty-Face went away, dragging his sack behind him. Me Dad said men like Dirty-Face were why I could never, ever go the park on me own and if I ever saw a man like that on the way home from school I was to run home as quick as I could, or I'd end up in his sack, just like Julie Sloane.

Julie Sloane mustn't have been able to run very fast. She lived in the next street to us and one day she went to the park on her own and she hasn't been seen since, even though there were loads of people looking for her and even though they put her picture in the *Echo*.

Julie Sloane didn't go to our school cos she was a proddy, but Miss Chambers said that made it even more important to say loads of prayers for her poor little protestant soul and so we lit loads of candles and everyone in school said the whole Holy Rosary at assembly, that's five hundred Hail Marys and I can't remember how many Our Fathers, but me knees had the same pattern as the floor by the time they let us stand up. I thought Julie was gonna come back after all those prayers but me Dad said we could say all the prayers we liked, but as long as there were men like Dirty-Face there'd always be little girls that never come home and if me and Debbie don't watch out we're gonna end up wiggling around in a sack at the bottom of the Mersey along with all the rest of the dawdlers.

Debbie's Dad told Debbie that there's another kind of bad men. He said it wasn't a man in a car or a man with a sack that took little Julie Sloane away. He said it was one of the ones that wear dark suits and helmets. Nasty horrible men that carry great big pairs of silver

4

handcuffs. Debbie's Dad says we should watch our backs cos other people can call them policemen if they want, but what they really are is pigs. I told me Dad what Debbie's Dad said, but he just said, "Well he would say that, wouldn't he?" and then him and me Mam laughed their heads off.

Sometimes we get fed up watching each other's backs so we go down to Piggy Monk Square. Piggy Monk Square is on the way to our school and it's dead good cos there's loads of falling-down houses that nobody lives in any more cos they've gone to live three bus rides away. Me Mam says the houses have been empty for over thirty years, ever since the war, and it's a crying shame that they don't knock them down, clear the rubble and rubbish away and build proper houses.

I hope they don't, cos me and Debbie love rubble and rubbish and we really love falling-down houses. There's lots of places to hide and we can play whatever games we want cos there's no old ladies moaning at us and going "Tut-tut-tut" and "You need a good wallop."

We'd be in for it if anyone found out we were playing down there so we don't go all that often and when we do, we only stay for a little while and we always, always, accidentally forget to tell our Mams and Dads.

We didn't go to Piggy Monk Square today cos Debbie's Mam wanted her to mind her little brothers, so she had to go straight home from school. We didn't go yesterday either, cos that was the day our class went on an outing, an outing to the museum.

A big bus came and collected us and it wasn't an ordinary bus. It was special cos it had bars on the windows to stop us falling out. We didn't have to pay either cos our teacher, Miss Chambers, had one big ticket for the whole class. When we got off the bus we had to line up, cross the road, then walk up loads and loads of steps. The museum is like a great big grey house, it's up really high and it's got big tall things called pillars to hold the roof up.

We had to be dead quiet in the museum. Miss Chambers kept her finger on her lips the whole time to remind us. We saw lots of old things but the best bit was the Egyptian room. That was a really special place cos that was where they kept the Mummies. Mummies used to be people just like us but now they're bandaged up. The one I liked the best was the biggest. He used to be a King or a Prince or something. His name was a big long word, I've gone and forgotten it now but I think it was Nuttytutkecks or something like that. He used to live in a place with lots of sand, like a great big beach only not a real beach cos Miss Chambers said it had no sea, no ice cream and no hot dogs.

Nuttytutkecks' bandages used to be lovely and clean and white but after he'd been left on his own in a Pyramid for a long time, his bandages went all yellowy-brown. When I looked really close at the bandages on his face I could see lots of stains, and I could see his nose and the top of his head under the bandages and they were all crinkly and black like he was made of coal. He looked like he'd been left in the yard for ages and ages. Miss Chambers said he'd been dead for thousands and trillions of years but he was preserved with lotions and potions.

6

Me Mam's got potions and lotions too and she puts them on her face when she's going to bed. She says they're to stop her getting old. I told her the Mummies looked really old and they had lotions and potions but she just said theirs weren't magic, not like hers.

Debbie's Nan used to look really old cos she never put magic potions or lotions on. Then one day she died and they put her in a big coffin-box, dug a big hole in the graveyard and put her in it. Debbie's Mam said her Nan wouldn't mind being under the ground cos she had gone to sleep, a big long sleep that lasts for ever. I'd mind. I don't want to get put in a wooden box under the ground when I die cos there'd be all worms wiggling down me ear holes. I want to get made into a Mummy cos then I can live forever.

Miss Chambers said that Mummies don't really live for ever. She said once they are dead they stay dead. But I know that's not true cos I got down on the floor in the museum to get a proper look at the Mummies and when I got up the King Mummy had turned his head, only a little bit mind you, only enough for me to see, cos I was the only one having a really good look. Dead people can't turn their heads so I knew the Mummies were only pretending. Anyway, Miss Chambers said it took the Egyptians ages to wrap bandages around the bodies and put preservatives on them and I don't care what she says, they wouldn't have done that for nothing.

When it was time to go, Miss Chambers gave us all a piece of paper to read on the bus. It had big pictures of Mummies and little pictures of their bandages and potions. When we got back to school Miss Chambers said we could all draw a picture of the best thing we saw in the museum. I drew a Mummy playing football and then I gave him lots of other Mummies to play with so he wouldn't be lonely. It was the best picture I ever did and all that mean Miss Chambers said was that Mummies can't move, never mind play football.

I told her I saw one moving, but she just said I've got me head stuck in the clouds too much. Well it's not fair, Miss Chambers went round the museum with her finger stuck to her mouth and her eyes stuck on us the whole time. She hardly even looked at the Mummies properly, so how could she know?

I wish I was in the museum now cos there's two policemen coming up our street. Their eyes are going from side to side, like as if they're looking for people to put the handcuffs on and take away. Dad says we need the police to look after us and that they have to look from side to side cos how else are they going to catch the robbers? I know me Mam and Dad don't lie but I know Debbie doesn't either, so what I do is I run in the house whenever I see them . . . just in case.

After tea I have to get washed, even if I'm spotless. We get washed in the kitchen. Me Mam puts the kettle on and gets the yellow bowl out from under the sink. In Debbie's house they have a tin bath and they put it in the front room by the fire. Poor Debbie has to get washed with all her horrible little brothers and they don't half smell.

After I'm all scrubbed and nice and shiny, me Mam always checks the back of me neck for muck and the back of me head for nits and if I'm all done then I can sit and watch the telly. Me Mam likes quiz shows cos she's dead clever and can answer lots of questions. She's good at crosswords as well and one time she got all the answers right and sent it off to a competition. She won a lovely picture of two hens and an egg. She hung it up on the wall over the telly and it was there for ages and ages till one night someone banged on the wall and it fell down and knocked over the goldfish bowl. Poor old Flipper hit the deck and that was the end of him. I miss him cos he never kept still. He just kept swimming around and around. I wish I'd known about the preservatives cos then me Mam might have let me keep old Flipper instead of putting him in a matchbox and sticking him in the bin.

After the quiz show I have to go to bed. Usually me Mam comes up and tucks me in and then me Dad comes up. If I'm still tucked in, he gives me a kiss on the cheek. They've forgotten to come up tonight though and I can't go asleep. I can hear them talking downstairs. It sounds like a little fight and pretty soon it will probably turn into a big fight. They're not shouting yet but I can hear them muttering and snapping and I know they're trying not to shout out loud. Any minute now they'll forget and they'll shout so loud that even when I put me fingers in me ears I'll still be able to hear them. They used to hardly ever fight but now they do it more and more. I don't like to hear them so I run to the window and make a little peephole in the curtains so I can watch what's going on in the street.

There's always something to see from my window and all the funny things happen at night. Like there's mad Harold and his wife, Skinny. Mam says they're on the ale. One night I saw Skinny pushing Harold along the street in a baby's pram. He's dead fat with a wobbly belly and Skinny's bones stick out and her skin is as white as sugar. I don't know how she pushes the pram with big fat Harold in it but me Mam said she's probably used to it. Harold was wearing a fluffy hat and laughing his head off. He had a baby's bottle full of brown stuff and was waving it around. Me Mam says they used to have a lovely little baby but it got sick and God came and took it up to Heaven one day so now they just pretend. I told me Mam they should have preserved the baby like the Mummies in the museum, then they could have kept it for ever and they wouldn't have to pretend any more, but me Mam said never, ever say anything like that again. I told her about the Mummy turning his head but she just told me to go and play.

There's no sign of Harold and Skinny tonight so I'm watching out for Stabber.

He doesn't live in our street, he lives up Lodge Lane, but he always comes down our street for a short cut. Stabber's big and lanky and he's got the biggest Alsatian dog you've ever seen, and he always wears a brown coat that's so long it sweeps the street as he's going along. He's got a really big pointy chin, so big you can see it coming round the corner before the rest of him. People with pointy chins are always the wickedest. All the witches in the books have got them too. He's got a funny walk as well. He always walks with one of his arms straight out in front of him, that's cos he has to keep tight hold of the dog's lead to try and stop it dragging him down the street.

I know Stabber's a psycho killer cos he's got great big pockets in his coat and when he walks by the lamp-post you can see the shapes of knives in them. Dirty great big ones too. He goes round stabbing loads of people and chopping them to bits. He doesn't have to bury the bodies either cos his brother's got a butcher's shop and he puts them in the mincer and turns them into sausages. Me Mam gets her sausages there but I won't eat them. They're full of chopped-up hearts and fingers. I told me Mam, but she just said I'd have to hurry up and learn that it takes all sorts and just because someone has a big chin doesn't mean they have to go round killing people and that his brother's shop did the best sausages from here to Speke. She would say that, wouldn't she? She loves sausages.

I have to be dead careful now cos Stabber's halfway down the street and I don't want him to catch me looking at him again. Last week he looked straight up at me and I could see his beady eyes staring at me like he was gonna get me and chop me up. He didn't get me cos I shut the curtains real quick and got me hand grenades from under the pillow. I love me hand grenades, they used to belong to Debbie's little brothers but they threw them at me and Debbie one day so we kept them and it serves them right. They're

not getting them back, not ever! I'm not so afraid of
Stabber now cos I know if he comes near me I could
blow him up. It'd be awful messy cos bits of his head
might get stuck all over me flowery wallpaper, but at
least he wouldn't get me. He's getting further up the
street, closer and closer, then when he gets to our house
he stops.

CHAPTER
TWO

I pull the curtains as close together as I can get them. I leave just enough space for one of me eyes to peep out. Stabber's standing still. His dog's doing a wee. When the dog's finished, he starts sniffing the wee and Stabber pulls him away. The dog doesn't want to go. He keeps pulling back on his lead. But Stabber puts both his hands on the lead and pulls really hard. The dog starts walking and Stabber follows but just as they go past, Stabber looks up at me. I get the curtains shut just in time.

It's gone dead quiet now. Mam and Dad have stopped arguing. It's funny the way it takes ages to fall asleep and then when you do you can't remember it. I was waiting for them to come up to tuck me in but the next thing is me Mam is shouting up the stairs to get me up for school.

I'm in a hurry to get out of the house today. We're going to ambush Uffo! He's me mortal enemy. He's in the next class up in school and he thinks he's hard, but he's not, he's chicken, cos he always says, "I'm gonna get me big brother on to you." I hate his guts and so does Debbie. He stinks like old rotten fish. We've been having a go at him for years and years and years. I can't remember how it started but it was his fault. Anyway it doesn't matter cos me and Debbie always win. When me Mam's not watching, I grab two eggs out of the fridge and leg it out the door. I call for Debbie on the way to school. She's not ready yet cos her Mam's doing her hair, so I have to wait. Her Mam gives me a dirty look and she says, "Sit there while I put our Debbie's hair in plaits. I don't want her getting nits now, do I?"

I can feel a beetroot coming. Just cos I got a note last week from the Nitty-Nora. Not my fault is it? Me Mam said nits only like clean heads, but that didn't stop her going mad when she first read the note. Anyway I know it was Uffo who gave me the nits. He took them out of his own head and threw them into mine.

That's why I robbed the eggs from our fridge. I'm gonna get him back on the way to school. That's if Debbie hurries up so we can get to the entry and hide before he goes past. When Debbie's Mam finishes doing the plaits she gets her to hold the ends while she goes to look for a bit of elastic and me and Debbie start whispering.

"Did you get some eggs then?"

"No, we haven't got any but I got a tin of tomatoes, will they do?"

"We haven't got a can-opener. Are they open?"

"Yeah, me Dad had some on toast last night."

Debbie's Mam comes back with the elastic, so we have to be quiet. She ties it round Debbie's plaits and points her squinty eyes at me. "Get going or you'll be late for school." As if I'm the one that made us late when she's the one that took ages doing the plaits!

14

We go tearing out of the house and rush down the street to hide round the corner on Uffo. We're only there a few seconds when he comes along. He looks made up with himself cos he's walking like he's hard. All the lads round our way want to look hard, so they all try and walk with long steps and their hands in fists.

He doesn't look hard for long cos I get him smack in the back of the head with the eggs and Debbie gets him wallop in the gob with the tomatoes. He looks like he's got sick all over him and he starts screaming, "You've 'ad it now! I'm gonna get you, soft girl!" He's got no chance, like I said, cos we always win, cos girls are the best.

We leg it all the way to school and we're nearly there when we hear the bell. We go like the clappers but we don't go fast enough cos Mister Shelby's standing behind the door when we get in and he makes us go in the late line outside his office. Now we've really had it cos we can hear the cane going up and down on someone and we know pretty soon it'll be us.

Robbie Renshaw's in the line just in front of us. He's always getting the cane. All he's got to do is . . . well nothing really. He just has to be there. Honest to God! He just comes into school and the next thing is, "You, Renshaw! Don't you look out the window!" And then it's whack, whack, whack with the cane. Or else, "Renshaw your tie's crooked!" Whack, whack, whack. It's not fair cos he always gets picked on. It's cos he's got afro hair, dead good cos it's all big and fluffy like a pop star. But Shelby doesn't like it, cos he doesn't like pop songs, only holy songs. Robbie told him that his hair won't go straight but Shelby doesn't believe him. Shelby said that if people like Robbie want to live in this country then they can jolly well do their hair properly like everyone else.

I give Robbie a tap on the shoulder. He turns round and he looks dead sad even though he hasn't been smacked yet. "What are you in the line for, Robbie?"

"Cos I forgot to bow me head when I said Jesus."

"Oh God! Oh Jesus! Oh Christ! That's a big sin. I think it's mortal!" I shouldn't have said that to him cos everyone knows mortal's the one where you burn in hell for ever and ever amen and now Robbie's sucking his lips, like he's gonna cry. Sometimes I'm dead, dead mean and dead, dead horrible.

There's a big gigantic late line today and Shelby comes out with his big old red face and gives everyone a dirty look. Paula O'Connor comes out behind him. She's crying her eyes out. No one really likes Paula cos she's got loads of snot and every time you look at her it comes dribbling out. But I feel sorry for her today cos the cane must have really hurt her. Everybody hates the cane and so do I.

I want to run away but Shelby'll only cane me even more when he catches me so I can't. Whenever I see the cane me spit gets stuck in me throat and there's none left for me mouth. Some kids start crying when they see it, but not me and Debbie cos we're brave.

Shelby must be in a rush cos he makes the three of us go in at the same time, then he grabs our shoulders and puts us in a little line in front of his desk. Robbie's first, then me, then Debbie. Shelby turns his back and stares out of the window. I think he's tired from a hard day's whacking and he's having a rest before he gets going again. Robbie turns round and looks at me and I turn round and look at Debbie. We've all got the same faces on, our lips pulled down to one side and our eyes squinched up to the other. That's what we all do when we know something bad's gonna happen.

All of a sudden Shelby puts his two big hairy hands behind his back and starts rocking from one foot to the other, and all he says is, "Mm, mm, mm." Then he spins round to look at us. He's just like a cowboy off the telly, except he doesn't shoot us. He just taps his hairy hand with the cane. When he's finished tapping, he pokes Robbie in the shoulder and says, "See you're here again, Renshaw."

"Yes, Sir."

"What have you done now, lad?"

"I forgot to nod me head when I said Jesus, Sir."

Shelby's eyes get littler and littler and he spins around again and starts hitting the wall with the cane.

"That's a terrible sin! Don't you know he died on the cross for you?"

"Yes, but I forgot."

Shelby goes purple except for two little white patches on each cheek.

"Yes? Yes? Is that all you can say? Don't they teach you anything where you come from, Renshaw?"

"But I come from round here."

He shouldn't have said that cos you can't answer back to the teachers. Shelby takes Robbie's hand and stares at it, then slowly turns it over to look at the back.

Then he wipes his own hand on his trousers as if it just got dirty. Robbie's hand is different than mine and Debbie's, first of all it's littler and second of all it's brown. The rest of him is brown too cos he's not white like us. Debbie's not allowed to play with brown kids so whenever she does she never tells her Mam. I can play with who I like as long as they've got clean knickers and don't say swear words.

Shelby lifts the cane real high in the air. Robbie's hand starts wobbling.

"Keep it still, Renshaw!" shouts Shelby.

"I'm trying, Sir, but it won't stay still," says Robbie.

That makes Shelby's face go snarly and he whizzes the cane behind him like the three musketeers and smacks it down really hard. It lands on the floor cos Robbie's hand moved again.

"I feel sick," says Robbie.

"I feel sick, Sir," says Shelby and now he's even more annoyed cos you always have to put Sir on the end when you say something to a teacher cos they're better than us.

"No Sir, really Sir, honest to God. I'm gonna be sick. I am!"

"You forgot to say please, Renshaw, you seem to forget a lot, maybe this will help you remember," says Shelby, grabbing his hand and swinging the cane behind him really fast. "Now say please." But Robbie doesn't answer and this time Shelby gets him so hard that he falls down and lies on his side on the floor. He puts his hands up his jumper to hide them but Shelby grabs him, stands him up, takes his hands out of his jumper and hits him again and again. He's got his aim straight now and he doesn't miss once. A bit of fizzy spit comes out of Shelby's mouth and he doesn't even wipe it off. The whole of Robbie is wobbling now, not just his hand. I can hear him breathing really loud. Shelby looks like he's never gonna stop, ever. I put me hands over me eyes. I don't want to look any more but then Robbie starts making funny noises so I move me fingers and look. Then he gets sick all over the floor, lots of sick with white and orange bits in it cos he must have had cornflakes and toast for breakfast. Shelby stops caning Robbie and looks at the ceiling for ages before bending down and putting his face close to Robbie's.

"Get to Miss Landers, stupid!" he shouts and another bit of spit comes out, falls off his chin and lands on his tie.

Miss Landers is the one who looks after us if we get sick in school. She's dead nice and she's got lovely puffy blond hair, pink shiny lips and cardies with lovely pearly buttons. She smells like talc and chicken soup. I'm glad Robbie's going to her cos she'll be really nice to him and bring him home to his mum. She might even give him a pink wafer. Robbie walks really slowly down the corridor and Shelby watches him till he's gone. I think he's forgotten about me and Debbie cos when he turns round to look at us his mouth opens up like he got a big surprise.

"What did you two do?" he asks.

"We were late, Sir," says Debbie.

I don't say nothing cos sometimes I just don't feel like talking.

"Put your hand out!" he says, pointing at me with the cane.

I can see Debbie looking at me and I know she wants me to do something brave like run away but I just stick out me hand cos I want to get it over with. I try not to look when he swings the cane back but I can't help it. All he does is just lift the cane a little bit so I only get a little tap that hardly hurts at all. Debbie gets the same, probably cos Shelby must have got worn out from hitting Robbie.

By the time we get to class it's time for milk and then out to the yard to play rounders. I like playing rounders but I don't feel like it today. I can't understand why Robbie's Dad doesn't come down to the school and stick up for him. Robbie says his Dad said it would only make things worse for him. Davey Rice's Dad came down one day after Davey got caned on the bum and he punched old Shelby right in the mouth! He told Shelby that if he ever laid a finger on Davey again he'd tear out both his eyeballs, rip his tongue off and break both his legs, and if he grassed him up to the coppers then he'd throw him to his cousins so they could finish him off. Davey never got hit again, not even a little tap, not even a little poke and not even a little push.

As soon as school is finished we go to our favourite house in Piggy Monk Square. We call it the Bommy cos the old ladies said it got bombed in the war. Out of all the falling down houses in Piggy Monk Square, the

Bommy is the best. It's the only one that's got a roof. It's got no proper doors or windows though, just the holes where they used to be. There's loads of rubbish as well, and today we're going to fix it up and make it really nice. The best room is one that's at the back. It's the only one that's still got some wallpaper on and we're gonna do that one first. It's full of planks of wood and bricks and we have to drag them all out of the way. The last thing we have to move is a big square bit with all jaggedy edges. I don't really know exactly what it is but I think it might be a bit of ceiling cos there's a hole up there that's the same shape. It takes the two of us ages to push it out of the way and when we finally do, there's a big metal ring underneath it.

We start pulling the ring but it's stuck to the floor. We pull really, really hard and up comes this big square piece of wood that was stuck to the ring. It turns out to be a trapdoor. I'm made up, cos in me favourite stories trapdoors always lead to really special places. Under where the trapdoor was there's a ladder leading down to a cellar. I love cellars as well. Cellars are the best! All the kids in stories have big, massive houses with attics and cellars and secret rooms, and if they haven't then they always have an Aunt Flora or Aunt Jemimah who lives in the country and her house is full of secret places and there's always treasure as well, lots of gold and jewels that used to belong to a pirate. I love stories with treasure at the end. Miss Chambers said the Egyptians used to put lots of treasure in with the Mummies but a lot of it got robbed. I hope there's lots of treasure in this cellar, but we can't find out cos our cellar's not like the ones in the stories. Our cellar is dark, really, really dark.

CHAPTER
THREE

Neither of us wants to go down there in the dark so we leg it to Fat Frank's shop to get matches. I never go to Fat Frank's shop cos he always stares at you all the time like as if any minute you're gonna stuff your pockets with his rotten old sweets. I don't want his old sweets, they've got fluff and flies stuck all over them, cos he doesn't keep them in a proper jar like Mister Abdul does.

"I'm not selling you two any matches," says Fat Frank.

"Oh go on Frank, me Dad sent us and he'll get a right cob on if he doesn't get his matches cos he won't be able to light his ciggy," says Debbie.

"On the slate?" he asks.

"Yeah, put them on me Dad's slate, not me Mam's," says Debbie, cos she knows her Dad won't remember what he put on the slate by the time Friday comes.

Fat Frank's afraid of Debbie's Dad. He used to be a boxer and he's still big with loads of muscles even though he's twenty-eight and old and past it now. He always says that he'd be rich and famous and on the telly if he had turned up for his big fight years ago instead of going to the pub with his mates and getting bevvied. He says he doesn't care cos he had a good laugh down the pub anyway.

Frank gets the matches and gives them to Debbie. She grins at me and whispers, "Tara, Fat Frank," but she must have whispered a bit too loud cos he starts to go mad and so we have to leg it. As soon as we get back to the cellar, we kneel at the top step to look down. I can't wait to go down and see what's there, but I don't want to go first. I can't tell Debbie that cos she'll only think I'm chicken.

"Go on then," she says.

"No, I always go first and anyway you've got the matches."

"Just cos I've got the matches doesn't mean I have to go first."

"You're not scared are you?" I know she hates anyone saying that.

"Course I'm not scared. I'm not scared of nothing."

So she climbs down the ladder and I follow.

Down in the cellar it's the blackest black I've ever seen and it's cold as well. The matches don't stay lit for very long and we have to strike loads of them and we still can't see much, just cardboard boxes and junk. I look around for treasure but I can't see any. It doesn't matter though cos anyone can see that this is the best hidey-hole in the whole wide world. It's perfect in every way except for one thing and that's the smell. It's a bit like the corner of me bedroom where the damp bit is, a musty smell that never goes away, even though me Mam's always spraying it with air freshener.

"I know," says Debbie, "this can be our hidey-hole."

"I already thought of that," I say, cos I did.

"Well you didn't say it though did you? I said it first," she says, all made up.

"I think we'll have to get a torch if we're gonna hide in here cos there's not enough matches . . . and I thought of that first."

"Evens," she says.

"Evens," I say, cos we have to come out evens cos we're bezzie mates.

We're just about to go back up the ladder when we hear a noise. Someone's coming.

"Quick Debbie, get in the corner and hide," I whisper.

So we run to the corner and make ourselves little. But then there's more noise and we hear a voice.

"Hey, you down there. What do you think you're doing?"

I can't see who it is cos there's a big light shining in me eyes, but it's a big man's voice and I don't like the sound of him and I don't like the sound of the sniffing noises he keeps making.

"This is the police! Get up here now! Come on, hurry up," shouts the voice and then there's another big sniffy noise.

"Oh Jesus Christ! What are we going to do? He'll take us away!" says Debbie.

We turn our faces to the wall so he can't see us.

"I can see you, stop hiding and come up here. This is the police."

We scrunch our mouths up cos we're not going to answer him.

"I'm telling you, get up here now! Or else I'll come down there and drag you up."

"Come on Debbie, we'll have to go up."

"No, I'm not going up, he'll get us."

"Come on Debbie we have to, there's no other way out."

I go first, I'm not as scared as Debbie cos maybe there's two kinds of policemen, horrible ones with handcuffs and nice ones who go looking for robbers. If this is a nice one then we're OK cos we're not robbers. Debbie comes behind me and she's going dead slow, like she never wants to get up the ladder. I stop and wait for her.

"I said shift yourselves! Hurry up!" Debbie just goes even slower. It takes us ages to get up the ladder and when we do, a bright light goes right in me eyes again, and I shut them quick cos it stings. Debbie grabs tight hold of me arm and I open me eyes again. The policeman is big and tall and he's shining his torch up and down us and he's sniffing and wiping his nose like he's got a cold.

"Well now you two, what have you got to say for yourselves?" He bends down and shines the torch in Debbie's face. She starts moving backwards and since she's still holding me arm I have to move as well. We can't get away from him though and the more we go backwards the more he moves closer. Soon we've both got our backs to the wall and there's nowhere else to go. Debbie pulls me arm. "Don't say nothing Sparra," she whispers.

26

"I heard that! Now, what were you doing down there?"

"Nothing," I say.

"Nothing," says Debbie.

"You were up to something, so come on, speak up!"

He's got a really scary voice and we both try and go backwards again but we just bang our bums off the wall.

"Cat got your tongues then? Right, where do you live?"

"Don't tell him," whispers Debbie.

"Do you think I'm deaf? Tell me where you live!"

"We're not robbers," I shout cos I hope he'll go away robber-hunting and leave us alone. He doesn't go away though. He grabs me by the hand and shakes me.

"Answer me!"

"You're not putting me in handcuffs!" I shout and I start squirming around trying to get him to let go of me arm. Debbie starts pulling me, trying to get me away from him and all of a sudden he lets go and we fall down. He starts laughing and puts his hand in his pocket.

"Take you away? Put you in handcuffs? Jesus Christ! Who's been telling you that? We don't put little kids in handcuffs any more, see."

Then he takes his handcuffs out of his pocket and grabs Debbie's arm. "Look, they'd be far too big for your little hands. You'd easy wriggle your way out, watch this."

He jangles the handcuffs around and he's just about to put them on Debbie's wrist when she starts to scream and scream. I want to scream as well but me voice suddenly goes away and I can't even whisper.

The copper starts laughing again and puts the handcuffs back in his pocket. "Now listen to me, I'm not going to do anything this time, but if I find you two in here again you'll get a lot worse than handcuffs, do you hear me? This place is dangerous. The bricks could fall on your heads and nobody would ever find you. Are you listening?"

We don't answer and he starts to sneeze and then he takes another hankie out of his pocket and starts blowing his nose again. Then we hear another man's voice, it's coming from his radio. He puts it to his ear and says to the man in the radio, "Right-o-will-do-over." Then he looks at us again and shakes his head.

"Listen, I haven't got time for you two little nutters. Clear off and go home. You know what'll happen if I catch either of you again, don't you?" He takes his handcuffs and jangles them in the air again and then he walks off, we can hear him laughing to himself as he walks away.

"What do you think he's laughing at, Debbie?"

"I think he's laughing cos he made us scared with his big handcuffs."

"Well I'm not scared any more, are you?"

"No I'm not scared either, we're not scared of that old Sniffer-cop with his rotten old handcuffs," says Debbie.

"That's good that, Debbie, that can be his name now. Sniffer-cop! Sniffer-cop!"

"Come on, leg it."

"I thought you weren't scared any more?"

"I'm not but me Dad'll murder me cos I'm dead late."

We run like the clappers till we get as far as Debbie's house.

"Come in with me, come on, me Dad won't kill me if you're there."

So I have to go in, don't I? I don't want to cos I'm late too, but I can't let me bezzie mate get hammered, so I go in.

Debbie's Dad doesn't go to work any more cos he says there's no point in trying when you live in this street. He just sits around the house most of the time watching the horse racing on the telly. Every now and then he peeps out the front door to see if there's any coppers coming up the street. If he sees one he goes "Pigs" and legs it out the back. Debbie says the coppers are always blaming her Dad for everything and when they can't find the real robbers they just come round and get him, to save themselves a load of bother.

When we go in he's lying on the couch, rolling a ciggy. He's got a little metal box for making them, and he usually does four or five at a time and leaves them sitting on the mantelpiece. He looks dead happy today and he's got a kind of funny grin on his face.

"Hiya Dad, sorry I was late, we had to help the teacher clean the blackboard," says Debbie.

"That's my girl, come 'ere and give us a kiss," he says, putting his lips in a kissy shape. Debbie goes over and he's being all nicey-nice. I can't believe it, especially when he starts being all nicey-nice to me as well. "There you are then Sparra, have you been a good girl today?" he says.

"I've been dead good, we both have."

"Come over 'ere then." I go over but I don't like the smell of pub coming off him. He reaches behind the couch, grabs a bottle and gets a big stinky swig out of it.

"All right then girls, since you've been good you can have a ciggy."

He takes two of his rollies and puts them in our mouths and then he even lights them.

He must be in a really good mood, one of his horses must have come first or something, cos he's never given us a ciggy before. We both start puffing and it's great.

We start walking round the room puffing and blowing and watching the smoke go up towards the ceiling. I start to get a bit dizzy though and I think Debbie is too. We both sit down and I feel a bit sick. Debbie's Dad starts laughing at us.

"Come 'ere," he says, "give us them ciggies, you're wasting them." He takes them and starts smoking the two of them at the same time. They're sticking out of each side of his mouth like two big Dracula fangs.

"Go on you, go home, your Mam'll be looking for you."

"See ya tomorrow Debbie," I say but she doesn't answer, just sits there looking at her feet, I think she's gonna be sick.

I try to sneak into the house real quiet, so I can run up the stairs and pretend I've been home for ages, but me Mam's standing by the door waiting for me. She's got her hands on her hips and she's not smiling so I know I'm in for it.

"Where have you been? You're late!" she shouts.

"I had to help the teacher clean the blackboard."

"Right then, hurry up and get changed. Your Auntie Mo's here, we've been waiting for you to come home so we can have our tea."

I start to feel sick again, and it's not from the ciggy.

CHAPTER
FOUR

I always feel sick when Auntie Mo comes round. She looks like a little witch with her black hair and black eyeliner and she always wears shiny trousers and big platform shoes to try and pretend she's tall and pretty like me Mam. She's not.

She's always going on about how horrible kids are today and how she's never gonna have any. Me Dad says it's a good job cos any poor little baby would take one look at her and go straight back where it came from. Course me Mam tells him to shush when he says things like that cos Mo's her sister. I haven't got any sisters but me Mam says it's the same as having a best mate cos you have to stick up for your sister the way you have to stick up for your best mate, especially if your sister's like Mo.

I heard me Dad saying that there's something wrong with Mo. She had an operation when she was a little baby. I think it was because her heart was in the wrong place cos that's what me Dad always says. Sometimes when she bends down you can see a scar, it starts at her neck but I don't know where it ends. But nobody will tell me properly cos it's a secret and they're afraid I'll tell. I wouldn't though. I wouldn't tell nobody, not one person. I'm really good at keeping secrets.

I go upstairs and take me uniform off really slow and I even hang it up in the wardrobe without being told. Usually I bung it on the floor, but the more time I spend up here in me room the less time I have to spend downstairs with Auntie Mo.

Me Mam comes to the bottom of the stairs and shouts, "Hurry up, Rebecca, your tea's out." So I have to go down.

Me Dad's sitting at the table grinning at me, but opposite him is Auntie Mo. She's sitting with her horrible old freckly arms folded and she's got a big gob on.

"Oh there you are, Rebecca. You're very late. I suppose you've been getting into trouble as usual," she says, her mouth twitching all over the place.

"She was helping the teacher clean the board," says me Mam.

"Are you soft in the head, Karen? It's gone six! It doesn't take that long to clean the friggin' blackboard."

"I had to help put the chairs away as well," I tell her.

"Listen Karen, someone's got to tell you straight. You're gonna have to do something about her cos she's making a holy show of you." Me Mam ignores her and me Dad just sticks a big lump of meat in his mouth so he can't say anything either, so she picks on me again.

"Listen to me, you. Are you still getting told off for day-dreaming and making up all that stupid stuff? When I was your age I worked hard in school and look at me now."

I look at her and look away real quick cos she makes me want to puke.

"Well Rebecca, what's wrong with you?"

I ignore her and start stabbing a spoon into the sugar bowl.

"Answer me when I'm talking to you."

She's just like that Sniffer. She wants me to say something and then she can pick on it and get even more annoyed. I keep on ignoring her and stare at the sugar. I can see her getting red out of the corner of me eye. I keep ignoring her and she goes beetroot. Now she's a little red witch instead of a black one.

"Answer me, you," she says.

"Leave it, Mo," says me Dad in a funny voice cos he's chewing at the same time.

"She's just ignored me, Brian."

"Well can you blame her? We're all trying to eat, Mo, give it a rest will you?"

Mam keeps staring at her dinner.

Mo leans across the table and pokes me right in the middle of me cheek. I hate that. I hate being poked more than anything, well apart from being pinched, I hate that too, I'd rather have a good smack any day. I'm not going to answer her now, not ever, not ever, ever.

"I'm asking you a simple question, answer me before I give you a good hiding."

"Mo, I'm warning you, leave off now! Look Karen, she's your sister, say something to her will you?" says me Dad.

"I want everyone to stop arguing so we can have our tea in peace," says me Mam.

"That's what we were doing until she caused trouble, or didn't you notice?" says me Dad.

"Don't you start as well, Brian," says me Mam.

Mo's eyes have gone so squinty that they're nearly closed and all you can see are the two black lines she always paints round them to try and pretend she's not ugly. Well she can paint all the black lines she wants cos she'll never be pretty and she knows it and she's dead jealous. Me Mam and Dad are staring at each other and while they're not looking Mo gives me another poke, this time in the shoulder. That's all she comes over here for, just to pick on me and give me a good poking. Well I'm sick of her now and I forget to stop me leg flying over to her leg and giving her a right good kick in her skinny little ankle.

She grabs her leg and jumps up. She starts hopping round the kitchen and shouting, "You little fuckin' bitch!"

"Well you're a wicked little witch!" I shout back.

"Karen! Did you hear the language out of your sister?"

"Karen! She just called me a witch."

"Mam it's not fair, she poked me."

"She kicked me!"

Me Mam rubs her forehead really hard with both her hands, then she lets out a big sigh and says, "Everyone just calm down, there's no need for it."

"Brian! Brian! What are you going to do? Are you a man or what? You can't let her talk like that. We'd have got leathered for that."

"You shouldn't have poked her, Mo. You've got no right. Has she, Karen?"

Mam picks up her fork and wallops it on the table. "Stop it everyone, I can't stand it. Why does this have to happen every single time we all sit down to eat?"

"That's easy Karen, it's because every time Mo comes here she starts picking on our Rebecca and then we end up fighting over it."

"Oh that's lovely that is. That's bleedin' nice. She kicks me and all you can do is blame me. That's typical! And what are you going to do, Karen?"

"Mo, be quiet for a minute, will you?" says me Mam.

"Oh, so you're blaming me as well now," says Mo.

"That's cos you are to blame, you stupid little cow!" says me Dad.

Mam puts her hand on me Dad's arm. "Oh Brian, for Christ's sake! Just ignore her, you know she can't help it."

"Like you do? Letting her think she can come in here and say what she likes, yeah Karen, that's really worked hasn't it?"

"This is great, this is. Are neither of you going to give her a good slap?" says Mo.

Mam puts her hands over her ears and closes her eyes. She looks really sad and I go up to her and put me arms round her cos I don't want her to cry. She lets me hold on to her for a minute then she stands up.

"Rebecca, go to bed," she says.

Mo's got a big smile on her ugly gob now cos that's exactly what she wanted. She always causes a fight and then when it starts she gets all happy. No one ever sees her smiling except me, that's cos Mam and Dad get too busy fighting. I go to bed cos I don't want me Mam to cry, but before I go I stick me tongue out at that Mo.

I run up the stairs to me bedroom. I look out the window for Stabber. I don't even bother hiding. I don't care if he sees me. I hope he does. I'll send him downstairs and tell him there's a juicy woman down there that'd make lovely sausages. I hope he puts her in the mincer, with her big gob going in first and I hope when she's turned into sausages she gets eaten up by the dog. But Stabber doesn't come past and I'm fed up.

I get into bed and start drawing little sausages on the wall. I put Mo's horrible face on them and draw little knives sticking into her eyeballs. I hear the front door slamming shut. Mo must be gone home, now she's done her dirty work. Mam and Dad start shouting at each other. They're dead loud. Not even bothering to pretend they're not fighting. I hear me Mam shout, "She's my sister, she can't help it and you know that."

"I don't care what's wrong with her, you shouldn't let her get away with it."

"What am I supposed to do?"

"Tell her straight. Tell her you don't want her coming round here no more."

"I can't do that, Brian. I'm the only family she's got. She's on her own since me Mam and Dad died. I promised me Mam I'd look after her. She's got nobody else. At least I've got you. Can't you understand that?"

"What about us, Karen? You're letting her wreck this family. Can't you see it? You have to sort her out or we'll end up finished."

37

"Oh right then, Brian. Blame me, everything's always my fault isn't it?"

"Yeah, well if it wasn't for her we could get away from this place, we could go and live in Ireland, but oh no, you won't leave Mo."

Me Dad's Dad came over here from Ireland years ago, got married to me Nan and they had me Dad. We've got loads of relations over there and one time we went on a holiday to see them. It was great cos first of all we went on a boat that took ages and we sat on the deck waving goodbye to Liverpool and bits of sea, and more bits of sea and then when we got fed up waving, we had corned beef butties, tea out of a flask and bananas for afters. Then we got off the boat and we had to get a funny-looking little bus with no upstairs and then we had to walk for ages, cos the bus didn't go all the way.

When we got to me Uncle's house we had loads of bacon and eggs and home-made bread with blackberry jam. After tea we went outside and me Uncle showed me a field. From far away it looked like there was lots of Dougal-dogs in the field but when we got closer they looked exactly like what they were, little mountains made of hay called haystacks. There was one in the corner that was smaller than the others and me Uncle said that was for kids like me to jump on, and as long as I didn't go near the other haystacks I could jump as much as I liked. I did too. It was the best fun, and by the time I'd finished the haystack was squashed flat. Me Uncle got a spiky thing called a pitchfork and put the haystack back together again.

He said that's so I could jump on it the next day too. That night I was itchy and me Uncle just laughed and said it was just the ticks from the hay. Me Mam didn't laugh though, cos she didn't like pulling them out of me legs with a tweezers and I didn't like it either. I soon forgot about the ticks though, cos the house was right by the beach. Me Dad taught me how to swim and we all went swimming every single day.

Me Uncle said we could all go back and stay for ever and he was even going to get me Dad a job, but me Mam said she didn't want to be stuck out in the middle of nowhere with just haystacks to talk to and she wasn't going to walk two miles for a loaf of bread either. Me Auntie said she could learn to make her own bread but me Mam said she wasn't going to start baking bread, she wasn't going to leave her friends and anyway she couldn't leave her sister all on her own and that was that.

They're shouting even louder now. I can hear me Mam's voice getting higher and higher.

"Oh Jesus Christ! Throw that in my face again, why don't you? Every time we have a row you go on about Ireland. I'm sick to the back teeth hearing about it."

"You had a great time when we went over, you know you did."

"But that was just for a holiday. I couldn't live there all the time."

"I don't see why not."

"Well it'd be different for you, Brian, you'd have all your family but I'd have nobody."

"You'd have me and our Rebecca."

"You know quite well what I mean, I wouldn't have me mates."

"Christ sake, you'd soon get to know people."

"I know but they're different, always going to Mass and all that . . . you know."

"So what? They were very nice to you when you were there."

"I'm not saying that, I know they were nice, it's just . . . it's different for you, you're a man. Anyway, you know I can't leave our Mo."

"Not her again, when are you going to stop worrying about her? She's not worth worrying about and she never was."

"Tell you what then, Brian, if it means that much to you, why don't you go then?"

"Maybe I friggin' well will then, if that's what you want."

"Well go on then, pack your bags if you want to. I'm not stopping you!"

"I will then!"

"Go on then!"

"I will!"

"What are you waiting for? I told you I'm not stopping you!"

I'm dying to run downstairs. I really want to stop him, even if me Mam doesn't, but I'm scared of making them even more annoyed. It's all gone quiet now but the door bangs. I run to the window and look out. I can see me Dad going down the street. But it's OK cos he hasn't got any bags with him. He can't go to Ireland with no clothes cos me Uncle is big and fat and none of his clothes would fit me Dad, so it must be all right. He must be just going to see a man about a dog, he does that sometimes when they've had a row.

I go downstairs. Mam is sitting by the table and she's crying her eyes out. When she sees me she rubs her eyes and pretends she wasn't crying. "Come on, love, I'll make us some cocoa."

She gets the little black pan and pours milk in and puts it on the gas. She can't be mad at me any more cos she only makes it with milk when I've been really good.

"I'm sorry for being so bad," I say.

"I know you are love but you shouldn't have kicked Mo. Look at all the trouble you've gone and caused and now your Dad's gone off in a huff as well!"

"I didn't mean to. Me Dad'll come back though, won't he?"

But she doesn't answer me, just keeps stirring the milk.

"Mam! Mam! Me Dad's coming back isn't he?"

She puts her hand on me shoulder and rubs it.

"Yeah love, I think he will."

But she's wiping her eyes and looking sad and I can't really believe her. I am gonna have to be really, really good from now on. I'm even going to be nice to that Mo. I'll do anything as long as me Dad comes back.

Me Mam starts making toast and she gives me some with the cocoa. Then she lets me sit beside her on the couch to watch telly. She puts a game show on and it's one of her favourites, but she doesn't even try to answer the questions, she just sits and stares and doesn't even drink her cocoa, not one little sip.

CHAPTER
FIVE

The light is peeping in through the gap in the curtains. I hear the milkman coming. The wagon makes a churning noise coming up the street and the bottles rattle like they're going to fall off any second. They never do though. I go downstairs and me Mam is sitting at the table drinking tea. Me Dad's not there but he never is in the morning cos he's on the early shift and goes to work before the milkman comes. There's nothing out for me breakfast so I just get a piece of bread and jam. Mam doesn't take any notice of me. She doesn't even tell me to go to school. I'm going to be really good though so I get ready and go myself.

I'm halfway down the street when Debbie comes running up beside me. She's been eating toast. I can see the crumbs around her mouth. Her hair is in two plaits again. I always have me hair in two bunches but now it's all loose and tatty cos me Mam forgot to do it. I'm going to get told off in school cos we have to have our hair tied up.

"Guess what me Dad did last night?" she says.

"Dunno, what?"

"He gave me another ciggy and he showed me how to smoke it proper."

"Did he? Was it good?"

"Dead good, he said if I'm good on Friday he'll give me a whole packet."

"How come your Dad was in a good mood then?"

"His horse came in and he got loads of money and we're gonna be dead rich. Me Mam says we're going to get carpets and everyone will be dead jealous."

"How much did he win?"

"Tons and tons and tons of money and guess what else?"

"What? What?"

"He gave me all his loose change and I went to the shop and I got this." She reaches in her pocket and takes out a little torch. It's gorgeous, real silver with a lovely little bulb that's shaped like a pearl drop.

"And look, guess what else?"

"What?"

She opens her school bag and pulls out a sheet.

"What have you got that for?"

"Me Mam says I can have it cos she's getting new ones. Look, there's a hole in the middle. Watch this!"

She puts her head in the hole on the sheet and it flaps around her like a huge cape.

"See, it's great isn't it? We can bring it down the Bommy and get dressed up with it." Debbie jumps up and down, she's made up cos she's got two new things.

"But what if that Sniffer-cop comes round again? He might get us."

"He won't. He thinks we're scaredy-cats and we're not, we're dead brave aren't we?"

She puts her little finger out and I put mine out as well. Then we link them together and shake them up and down to prove we're bezzie mates.

The first thing we have to do in school is religion. Miss Chambers goes on about all the different sins you can do. There's loads. You don't even have to do nothing! You can just think up some really wicked thoughts. That's me in trouble anyway cos I'm always having really wicked thoughts. Like now, when we're saying our prayers. I keep thinking Miss Chambers might fall over and we'll all laugh. Then she'll have to walk on big crutches and she won't be able to get in the classroom door cos if she takes her hands off the crutches to push the door open she'll fall over. Sometimes I imagine Stabber getting her and frying her up in a pan, covering her in ketchup and eating her all up. That'd be great cos we'd get off school for ages while they found a new teacher. Mind you I wouldn't really like that, not really, really, cos Miss Chambers is OK for a teacher. She never wallops us hard and she's better than that Sister Mary that we had last year. She had a moustache and she was always trying to rub it off with her finger. She used to walk around the class with a ruler in her mouth so she could smack us dead quick whenever she wanted.

"Rebecca! I'm asking you a question!"

Miss Chambers is standing beside me. I didn't see her coming.

"Day-dreaming again, Rebecca?"

"Sorry, Miss."

"Well, what's the answer?"

I can't tell her what the answer is cos I don't know what the question is.

"I asked you what the sermon was about at Mass on Sunday, Rebecca."

She would ask me that now wouldn't she? I haven't got a clue cos we only go at Christmas. She makes me stand with me face turned to the wall. She says I'm an example. I'm always being the example. It's not fair. I peep round when she's not looking and Debbie waves at me. I wave back and Miss Chambers catches me.

"Right that's it, Rebecca, you can jolly well stay in at playtime for that."

It takes ages for the day to go by when I haven't got playtime. Debbie keeps looking at me and grinning so I know she can't wait either. When the bell goes we're the first out the door.

We want to get there quick cos we don't want to be too late home and get into more trouble. When we get to Piggy Monk Square we look around everywhere to make sure old Sniffer's not around and then when we're sure he's not, we run into the Bommy and down into the cellar real fast. Debbie's torch is great and we can see lots of things in the cellar that we couldn't see yesterday. The walls are just bare brick and they feel dead rough and crumbly when you touch them. There's a mattress with springs poking out, an ironing board, a pile of old bricks in the corner and a little statue of an eagle with the paint peeling off. It's great to be able to see everything with the torch cos now we know where the smell's coming from. It's the old mattress.

"We better go home now, Sparra," says Debbie.

"OK, but let's just bring the mattress up and throw it out cos it stinks and we don't want anything smelly spoiling our hidey-hole."

The mattress isn't too heavy, not for the two of us, but it's big though, bigger than us. I go first up the ladder, holding the top bit, and Debbie follows holding the bottom. Just when I get near the top step it slips from me hand and falls, it nearly squashes Debbie. We have to go back and start again. This time Debbie takes the top bit and I take the bottom and we go nice and slow. It takes ages to get it up the ladder. Even with me pushing it and Debbie pulling and it's really hard to get it through the trapdoor. In the end it bends in the middle and at last it goes through.

The cellar looks even more special now without that stinky mattress. We make a little table out of the bricks and put the eagle on it. It won't stay straight so we put another brick behind it to stop it falling again. Debbie gets the sheet out and rips it in two where the hole is. "I know, let's play ghosts," she shouts and gives me half the sheet. The sheet is really thin and there's a tear at the end. I pull it and a whole strip comes away. It looks just like a bandage, a big long bandage, a big long Mummy bandage.

"Let's play Mummies! Look, it rips dead easy," I shout, ripping another long strip off.

We both start ripping the sheet and soon we've got a whole pile of bandages.

"Right Debbie, you bandage me, then I'll bandage you."

"OK." She starts trying to bandage me, but she can't do it properly and hold the torch and I can't hold the torch cos I've got to keep me arms still.

Debbie puts the torch on our little table and fixes it so the light shines on me. She's just about to come back and get started on me leg when suddenly the light flashes right in me eyes.

"What did you do that for, Debbie?"

"What?"

"Put the light in me eyes."

"I didn't."

The light starts moving really fast around the cellar. We both look at Debbie's torch but it's sitting still on the brick table.

"You two again!"

It's Sniffer-cop! Debbie grabs the torch off the table and turns it off. I grab the bandages and we run to the corner.

"Come on you. I know you're down there, I saw the torch. I warned you two yesterday to stay away from here."

"Oh God now we've had it! What are we going to do?" whispers Debbie.

"I dunno!"

"Oh God! He'll put us in the handcuffs."

Sniffer shines the light right in Debbie's eyes.

"Dead right! I've got special little-girl-sized handcuffs today. Now come on, get out of there or I'll come down and put them on you."

He lowers his face through the trapdoor, he looks dark and shadowy, like a ghost. Neither of us moves.

"Right then you two, I'm gonna count to ten. If you're not up here by the time I'm finished, I'm gonna come down there and you're getting the cuffs!"

Sniffer-cop makes a noise like he's sniffing a big lump of snot up and down his nose. That gives Debbie the giggles and even though I'm scared, I catch them as well. Something starts rattling. It's the handcuffs! Me giggles go away all of a sudden, so do Debbie's.

"Right, that's it. One, two, three, sniff, four, five, sniff, six, seven, sniff, eight, nine, ten . . . That's it, you've had your warnings."

The rattling noise stops and we hear his footsteps coming down the ladder. Debbie runs behind me to hide but then I run behind her cos I want to hide as well. Suddenly Sniffer shouts "Shit!" His leg goes flying out and he goes crash bang wallop all the way down the ladder. He lands right on the place where the mattress would have been if we hadn't thrown it out. His torch hits the wall, spins round and round, then stops with the light shining straight at Sniffer. He doesn't seem to notice, cos he just lies there and doesn't move an inch.

CHAPTER
SIX

We wait for him to get up but he doesn't. He doesn't open his eyes or blink or anything.

"Come on, we'd better get out of here," says Debbie.

"We can't leave him, we have to try and help him," I say, even though I want to run away.

"Don't be soft, Sparra, he'll get up in a minute. It's probably a trick to get us to go close so he can grab us and put the handcuffs on. We have to go or else we'll get the blame. They're always blaming me Dad for nothing and they'll blame this on us if we don't get going." Debbie starts to go and I grab her arm.

"But look at his leg, it's sticking out the wrong way. How's he gonna get back up the ladder? We'll have to tell someone."

"We can't tell anyone, whatever we do, we can't tell. Me Dad says never tell nobody nothing."

"OK, but maybe we could get him up the ladder. At least he'll be able to get away himself then."

Debbie walks around Sniffer. She gets the end of her plait and puts it in her mouth to have a suck the way she does sometimes when she's scared.

"OK, we'll get hold of an arm each."

We try and drag him. We pull like mad but he's really heavy and we can only move him a bit.

"We'll have to leave him here Sparra, we'll never get him out, he's too big."

"We can, we got the mattress up the ladder didn't we? We just have to pull harder."

We pull again, really hard, but we still only move him a few inches. We're both puffing like we've been running and Debbie suddenly stops pulling. She spits her plait out of her mouth.

"Tell you what, get his legs."

"We can't pull his sore leg."

"He's asleep, he won't mind."

I get his good leg and Debbie takes his broke one. We both start pulling again but then we hear a funny noise, a bit like when you step on a twig in the park, only louder.

"Oh God! What was that?"

"I dunno." Debbie lets go of his leg.

"I think we've gone and broke him a bit more."

"No we haven't."

"We have Debbie, that's what the noise was."

"Well, we didn't do it on purpose."

"I know but if the rest of the coppers come they'll think we did."

"Well come on then, let's go before they come."

"We can't, what if he dies or something? It would be our fault."

"Oh you can't die from breaking a leg. Me Dad got his arm broke once in a fight and he didn't die. He says he broke both the other fella's arms and he didn't die either."

Debbie gets on the ladder. "Come on Sparra, we have to go! Come on!"

I don't want to leave him here, but I don't want to stay either cos I don't want to get the blame and I don't want Sniffer's mates coming and catching us and taking us away. Debbie's got halfway up the ladder and she's waiting for me to follow her. I'm stuck, me legs want to run up the ladder and get away but the rest of me won't move.

"Hurry up, we have to leg it, you know what'll happen if they catch us — please Sparra."

"I can't, me legs won't go."

Debbie comes back down and grabs me hand.

"Sparra, we have to, if we stay here any longer we'll never get home, they'll catch us and then we'll never see our Mams or Dads again."

Me legs start moving and before I know it we're outside.

We start running and we don't stop till we've got all the way to the main road.

Debbie's face is all red. One of her plaits has come undone so one side of her hair is loose. Her socks are falling down and she leans against a phone box to fix them. Suddenly she stands up straight and puts her hand over her mouth.

"I haven't got me torch. I must have dropped it on the way out. I have to get it."

"But we can't, we can't go back, not with him there."

"I have to get it Sparra, you know me Mam'll go mad if I've gone and lost it already."

She sticks her lip out like she wants to cry.

I look at the phone box and see that it's empty.

"I know, let's ring an ambulance and tell them to go and get Sniffer."

"They won't take any notice of us, they'll just tell us to get off the phone."

One time Debbie's Dad punched her Mam in the mouth and Debbie said all her Mam's blood came squirting out like a big fountain. Debbie ran to the phone box to get an ambulance, but when she told them where she lived they told her to get off the phone and stop messing cos they were sick and tired of it and when she got home she got a smack from her Mam for telling tales outside. I want to try it though, in case someone nice answers and anyway I'm only going to tell them where Sniffer is, nothing else.

"We can try and see, come on."

"They won't listen to you, Sparra, honest to God."

I go in and she follows me. I pick the phone up and listen, but I can't hear anything.

"It's not working," I tell Debbie.

"Bang it on the side, that's what me Mam always does."

So I give it a bang on the side and the next minute the door opens and there's this old lady looking in at us. She starts wagging her finger.

"Oi! You two! Stop wrecking that phone box!"

"We're not, we're trying to fix it," says Debbie.

"No you weren't, I saw you banging it, now come on, clear off."

She gets hold of us and pulls us out.

"Where do you live? I'm gonna go and tell your Dads on you."

We look at each other and Debbie shouts, "Leg it!" And the next minute we're up the road. When we get as far as the pet shop we stop and look back. The old lady's still wagging her finger but she's not running. That's the best thing about old ladies, they can't run.

"See Sparra, I told you they won't listen to us. Now I'll never get me good torch back."

"He might be gone tomorrow."

She's just about to say something when all of a sudden there's a loud squawk.

We both turn round. It's coming from the pet shop window. It's a big green parrot in a tall cage. He's hopping up and down a little parrot-ladder. He seems happy but I think he's sad really, probably cos he really wants to fly and the cage is too small.

The parrot squawks again, like he's trying to talk. I heard parrots can talk but I can't understand what this one's saying. He goes to a tray of seeds and eats some. His beak looks really sharp, sharp enough to bite a finger off. Debbie taps the window and the parrot flaps his wings, then runs to the top of the ladder. He seems to want to play with us, so we take turns tapping the window and watch him hopping up and down the ladder. Suddenly the parrot stops moving. I tap the window again but he takes no notice, he's staring at something behind us.

We turn round to see what and there, right behind us, is Uffo and his big brother Lippo. He's got hold of Debbie's plait and then he grabs me hair as well. Stupid hair, me Mam wanted to cut it when I got the nits that time but I screamed blue murder and me Dad stopped her in the nick of time so now I've got lots of hair, enough for Lippo to hang on to. It feels like it's being ripped off me head. Uffo's standing there, watching everything with a dirty great big smirk on his face. "I'll get you for this, Uffo!" I shout.

"Yeah," shouts Debbie. "You let go of us or me Dad'll kill you!"

"No he won't," says Lippo, "I battered him last week. I can take him any day."

Then he digs his fingers into me arm. He looks like Uffo, only bigger and even more ugly cos he's gawpy looking with straggly hairs on his chin and he goes round with his big fat lip hanging down cos he's too stupid to shut his mouth.

There's an entry beside the shop and he pulls me and Debbie into it. The entry smells horrible, like poo and rotten meat. Lippo throws Debbie on the floor and says, "Sit on her, Uffo." Uffo sits on Debbie so she can't get up. Then Lippo takes a pair of scissors out of his pocket. He puts them on me face and I can feel how cold they are. I keep wriggling and wriggling, but he's got me by the arm and I can't get away.

"Is this the one that started it, Darren?"

"Yeah, but you're not gonna stab her are you?"

"No, don't be soft, I'm gonna do something better. Something she's gonna remember every time she looks in the mirror."

"Oh no, don't. I didn't mean you to do that! Stop it, Dave!"

Uffo stands up and starts pulling on Lippo's arm. Debbie starts getting up.

"Friggin' hell don't do that, don't cut her with the scissors!" Uffo's jumping up and down, shouting at Lippo.

Lippo pushes Uffo. I start to scream and scream but he picks up a chip paper off the ground and stuffs it in me mouth. He grabs a piece of hair and pulls it hard. Then he gets the scissors and cuts it off. He sits back holding me hair and laughing. "See, that's what you get for telling everyone you got nits off our Uffo and for getting him with eggs and tomatoes. Now if you ever do that again I'll cut the fuckin' rest off! Got it?"

Debbie starts thumping Lippo as hard as she can, but Lippo just grabs her two arms and throws her back down on the floor. He's just about to cut her hair as well when someone else comes into the entry.

CHAPTER
SEVEN

"Oi you! What the hell are you doing? Leave her alone!"
I spit the chip paper out. It's Stabber! He pulls Lippo
up, grabs his mouth and squeezes really hard. Lippo
makes glugging noises. Stabber swings him round by
his mouth and all of a sudden lets go, so Lippo goes
flying down the entry. He gets up and starts running.
Stabber's dog starts growling and nodding his head at
Uffo.

Uffo starts to walk backwards. "It wasn't me, it was
him!"

Stabber moves towards him. "Why aren't you
running?" Uffo starts running like the clappers.

Stabber looks at me and Debbie and he says, "Are
you OK?"

But we take off. He hasn't got a sack or a dirty face
but he's not called Stabber for nothing and we don't
want him to get us. We can hear him shouting after us,
"It's all right, come back."

No chance.

When I get home, I go straight in the kitchen to look
at me hair in the mirror. There's a short bit at the front
now. I pull another bit of hair round from the side to
hide it. Me Mam's at the cooker. She's stirring the pan

so hard that I can hear the spoon scraping the bottom. She doesn't look at me or tell me off for being late so I know there's something wrong. I look for me Dad's coat on the hanger under the stairs. It's not there. He should be home by now cos when he's on the early shift he usually gets in before me.

"Mam, where's me Dad?"

She just keeps stirring the pan.

"Mam! Mam!"

"Go and get changed, Rebecca, I'm busy."

She picks up the pan and bangs it on the cooker so I do what she says.

I'm dying to tell her what's happened but if I tell her, she'll go mad cos I was down the Bommy. I want to prove that I'm good, really good, then nobody will be mad any more.

I go upstairs and get changed. I lie on me bed. I just want a little lie-down but I can't keep still. Me stomach feels like it's full of little ants all jumping about. I look at me curtains. They look different. It seems like the flowers have got big staring eyes and they're all looking at me. I look at the ceiling instead but that's even worse cos there's big black branches coming out and they're getting closer and closer. I jump up and go back downstairs.

There's a plate of chicken stew on the table. I love chicken stew and so does me Mam. But there's only one plate. Mam's just sitting there staring at the salt cellar. She hasn't got anything to eat.

"Aren't you having some dinner?"

She won't answer me cos she's playing a funny game. It's called "Pretend Rebecca isn't here". I don't like this game but she won't stop. The salt cellar is a bit like an Egyptian Pyramid only with stripes on. I suppose it's quite nice really but we've had it for ages, so I don't know why me Mam keeps on looking at it now as if she's never seen it before.

I pick it up and put it on me lap where she can't see it any more. I want her to say something, even if it's bad, but she doesn't say a single word and now she's staring at the table. It's like quiet time in school. I hate quiet time and before I can stop myself I shout out.

"Mam! Mam! Something happened to me on the way home from school!"

All she does is make a big sigh.

"Mam listen! Listen!"

I get up and hold on to her arm.

"What? What now?"

She's not pretending I'm not here any more, but she looks quiet-mad. I hate quiet-mad cos sometimes that's worse than shouting-mad, so I don't tell her.

"I said what?"

"Nothing."

"I hope you weren't playing in those old houses."

"No, Mam."

"What then? You weren't fighting were you?"

"No, Mam. I saw a parrot in the pet shop."

"Oh, that's nice love," she says.

"It was green," I tell her, but it feels like even though me mouth's doing the talking, it's not me that's telling it what to say, so I squash me lips together and push me stew round the plate. I don't feel like eating it cos the little ants are still running round me stomach.

"Eat your dinner, Rebecca."

I put a spoonful in me mouth but as soon as I do I get sick. All over me lap. I can't stop and I know it's making a terrible mess but it just keeps on coming out.

"Oh, Jesus Christ!" says me Mam.

She's really looking at me now. She brings me into the kitchen and fills the yellow basin with water.

"What did you eat in school today?"

"Nothing."

"Well something's upset your stomach. Maybe it's a bug."

Then she takes me clothes off and washes me. I always do it myself, except when I'm sick. She uses pink soap. She's nice and gentle and it makes me feel better. She puts a clean nightie on me as well, even though it's not Saturday. She gives me a hug and it's all nice cos I didn't think I'd be getting hugs any more, but then she starts to squeeze me and she's forgotten I'm only little and it feels like I'm going to break. I have to pull away and when I do I see that her eyes are all watery.

"What's the matter? What are you crying for?"

"I'm not crying."

"You are crying. I can see the tears."

"Well I'm just a bit, sort of tired, that's all, just tired."

"Why are you crying cos you're tired? What's the matter? Where's me Dad?"

She shakes her head and stops crying.

"He's got to work extra shifts, he'll be home in a few days."

I don't know whether to believe her or not. I want to, but even when me Dad does overtime he still comes home. But me Mam doesn't tell lies, so maybe it's OK. Maybe she's just sad cos she misses him. It's not as if they fight all the time, sometimes they're all lovey-dovey and kissy-huggy. I miss him too but then if he's doing all that extra work he'll probably buy lots of nice things, maybe we'll get new carpets like Debbie. That'll be great cos then we'll be the same. We like being the same. Me Dad might even bring home chocolates for me Mam and then she'll be really happy.

We watch telly for a bit but there's nothing good on and she turns it off. She doesn't read the paper or even put the radio on, just sits there. I want to stay up and read me comic but she won't let me. She puts me to bed and I get me book out. I love this book cos it's all about a girl called Emma. She's got a magic horse that she goes all over the highways and byways and laneways and pathways on. She's always saving people cos she lives in a forest and people are always falling down mountains and into rivers and she gets her magic horse to pull them out. She's a bit like me, sometimes she gets blamed for things she doesn't do cos her enemy, the wicked Julietta, plays nasty tricks. But Emma is dead clever and sorts everything out and horrible Julietta always ends up getting a million lines or else she falls into a big pile of magic poo and everyone laughs at her.

60

I give me Mam the book to read to me but she just puts it on the floor and tucks me in. She doesn't even say goodnight when she goes back downstairs. It's like she keeps forgetting I'm there. I get Ellie from under me pillow. Ellie is an elephant. He's grey with fluffy pink ears and I've had him since I was born. He used to have a little yellow jacket but I lost it. Now he's got no clothes and he looks cold cos he's got little bald patches where his fur has rubbed off. I want to keep Ellie for ever, even when I'm too old for toys. Only thing is, he won't live for ever if his fur keeps coming off, so I'm going to make him into a Mummy. I tiptoe into Mam's room and get lots of tissues from the box on the dressing table. I take her lotion as well cos Ellie's going to need preservative if he's going to live for ever. I wrap the tissues round and round until he's all covered up, then I put a blob of Mam's lotion on them and rub it in. Ellie looks just like the Mummies in the museum except that he's only little and he's got nice clean bandages and he smells lovely. I tuck him in beside me and put the covers over him.

When I wake up me mouth is full of bits of tissue. I must have been sucking Ellie's ear. When I get downstairs Mam hands me a piece of toast with no jam on it or anything. She sits down like she's tired even though we've only just got up. I don't want to make her even more tired so I try to fix me own hair in a bunch but it's in a big tangle and the short bit at the front won't go in for me.

Debbie's waiting for me halfway down the street. Her two plaits are dead neat and there's not one little bit sticking out. We don't want to go in the late line again so we go straight to school as quick as we can without stopping, not even to talk to each other for a minute. I'm glad cos I don't want to talk, and I specially don't want to talk about Sniffer. We get to school before the bell even goes.

We're doing sums today and Miss Chambers is writing them all out on the board. We have to copy them down in our books and then we have to work out the answers. I write them all out but I can't remember how to get the answers, so I just write them out again. Miss Chambers goes round the class checking everyone's work and when she gets to me she says, "Why didn't you put your hand up, Rebecca? All you have to do is put your hand up if you don't know how to do the sum."

"Sorry Miss." But it's OK cos she's nice today, and she tells me how to do every sum and in the end I get them all right and I get a gold star. I can't wait to get home and tell me Mam, that'll cheer her up. She might even get cake for our tea.

At lunchtime the dinner ladies come and take us over the road to the dinner centre. I hate school dinners. School dinners come in either great big tin cans full of sloppy stew with hard bits or big long trays full of gristle-meat pie. There's always wet mash to go with it, and we have to queue up while the dinner ladies take the biggest spoon you've ever seen and plonk the slops down on our plate. Debbie always eats hers cos she doesn't mind it but I never do, not never.

One of the dinner ladies comes over and she sees I'm not eating. It's Miss Jeffries. No one likes her cos she's always got a gob on and she wears a wig. Underneath she's baldy. She thinks we don't know but she's stupid cos we can see it slipping around on her head. She taps me on the hand.

"You again? Eat your dinner or I'll report you to Mister Shelby."

"Miss, I'm not hungry."

"I said, eat it now."

Debbie puts her fork down. "She's not hungry, Miss."

Miss Jeffries points her finger at Debbie's nose. "Nobody asked you, keep your nose out. And you, Rebecca, eat up!"

"No. I don't like it."

"Spoiled, are you? Too good for school dinners, are you? Well we'll see about that."

She picks up a spoonful of wet mash and tries to shove it in me mouth. I squash me lips together so it misses and falls off the spoon. She grabs me ear and waggles it about. It hurts but I keep me mouth shut.

"Open your mouth!"

I squash it shut even more. She grabs me nose and I can't breathe. Me mouth comes open by itself and quick as anything she shoves the mash inside. She squeezes me nose even more but I keep the mash at the front of me mouth, and when she lets go I spit it out and it goes all over her soppy old frilly jumper.

"You dirty little bug . . ."

She grabs me by the shoulder and starts trying to drag me away, but I hold on tight to the table and even though she's pulling as hard as she can, she can't get me. Debbie jumps up and holds on to me, so no matter how hard Miss Jeffries pulls, she can't get me off the table. All the other kids are giggling and pointing, and Colin Owens who's the naughtiest boy in our class gets a big spoonful of wet mash and throws it at Miss Jeffries. It sticks in her wig and everyone laughs some more. Miss Jeffries goes like a beetroot and shouts across to the other dinner ladies, "Go and get Mister Shelby! Quick! Quick!" All the kids suddenly stop giggling and they all put their heads down. That's what we always do when we know Shelby's coming, except Debbie. She sticks her chin out and she shouts at Miss Jeffries in a really loud voice.

"Go on, get Mister Shelby then. I'll tell him how many of them pies you take home to your own house. Everyone knows you're a dirty robber, we can see them sticking out the top of your bag. Go on then, you go tell on us to Mister Shelby and I'll go tell on you."

Miss Jeffries lets go of me and folds her arms. The other dinner ladies are coming over but she puts her finger on her lips and waves at them. She walks really fast to the far side of the dinner centre and starts pouring water into beakers on the little kids' dinner table. I feel sorry for the little kids cos I can see her banging their beakers down and I know she's going to pull their ears, but I feel better too cos now I don't have to eat that rotten dinner.

64

When dinner's over we go out to play. Me and Debbie play walking in a circle as fast as we can. All our class join in cos it's a great game. Whoever is the last to get dizzy and fall over is the winner and the others all have to give the winner a sweet. Round and round and round I go cos I'm the leader. Soon loads of kids are falling over and then there's just me and Debbie, then she falls down but I keep going for ages and ages. I don't really feel like I'm getting very dizzy, but all of a sudden I am really, really dizzy and I try to stop myself running so fast but I can't and the next thing is I go plonk on the ground and all the kids are running around me cheering. I get three flying saucers, a packet of Swizzles and a sherbet dab.

The bell rings and we go back to class. Miss Chambers tells us a long story about Eskimos. They live in snow houses called Igloos and they keep warm by wearing big furry coats. It's always snowing where they live. They've only got fish and bears to eat cos there's no shops and there's no chippies. They don't go to school so there's no cane, no dinner ladies and you can play in snow all day. I wish I could be an Eskimo.

We go past the Bommy on the way home. Debbie stops but I keep going.

"Come on Sparra, I want to get me torch," she says.

"I don't want to, I don't want to be late," I tell her but she catches me hand and pulls me back.

"Sparra, I have to get me torch. I can't go on me own. You're supposed to be me bezzie mate."

"What if he's still there, Debbie?"

"He'll be well gone. Come on, let's just run in and check. I don't want to be late either, cos I don't want to be kept in, specially not tonight."

"Tonight?"

"Yeah, you know, the street party. You haven't forgotten, have you?"

I had forgot! Our street has a party every year. Not cos it's someone's birthday or anything but just cos it's the best street in Liverpool. We always have a bonfire and fireworks and loads of lemonade and crisps and when we've had that, we make toast on the bonfire.

"Come on Sparra, let's just peep in."

"All right then." I know she won't give in.

Debbie's torch is right by the trapdoor. She must have dropped it when we started to run. We don't go right down the ladder, we stay at the top and listen, but we can't hear a single thing so Debbie shines the torch down into the cellar.

CHAPTER
EIGHT

We can see a dark shape on the ground. Sniffer's still there and he's in exactly the same place.

"Oh God, Debbie, what are we going to do? He's dead."

"No, he's not."

"Look, he's not moving."

"We'll have to go down and see, come on."

We climb down into the cellar. Debbie goes first and shines the torch on his chest and we can see it going up and down.

"See! He's not dead," she says.

"What'll we do?"

His walkie-talkie thing is sticking out of his pocket so I pick it up and put it to me ear but I can't hear anybody talking. Debbie grabs it and listens.

"It's broke," she says. "It must have broken when he fell down the ladder."

She shakes it around for ages but it still doesn't work. I grab it back and give it a quick thump, like me Dad does to the telly sometimes when the picture goes funny. Still nothing. It looks OK though, maybe we're just not doing it right. I press all the little buttons. Nothing happens. We both bend down and have a really good look at Sniffer. I don't like him lying there all quiet like that, it's nearly as scary as when he was shouting at us, so I give him a tap on the shoulder with just two of me fingers. "Wake up. Wake up." But he doesn't.

Debbie takes the walkie-talkie and shakes it some more.

"Maybe he needs a drink of water, on telly when someone won't get up they always give them a drink of water."

"We haven't got any water."

"We'll just have to leave him then, maybe he'll wake up by himself."

"But what if he doesn't?"

"He will. Anyway, Sparra, we didn't ask him to follow us and we weren't robbing or nothing so he didn't even have to come after us. He could have just left us alone. We weren't doing nothing wrong. Come on, let's go." Debbie stands up.

"We can't just leave him. It's perishing cold in here. He might . . . die."

"No he won't," says Debbie. "It's not even snowing and the Eskimos don't die of the cold and they live in the coldest place in the world."

"But they have furry coats and Igloos."

We both look at him. He's got his jacket and trousers but his helmet's fell off.

I pick it up and try and put it on his head. I can't get it to go on properly so I try and lift his head up. All of a sudden he turns and looks at me.

"God!"

"Jesus!"

"He moved!"

"Run!"

Sniffer tries to lift his head and says in a whispery voice, "Don't go, wait, give me my radio. I think my leg's broke and I can't move my back, it's . . ."

His eyes are open but they're sort of funny, all red and sore looking and his lips are all cracked. Debbie's got the arm pulled off me trying to get me away. I want to go, but I think we should help him even if he is a horrible old copper.

"Well, if we give you the radio you have to promise not to put handcuffs on us and take us off to prison," I say.

"I promise, please give it to me."

Debbie puts the radio behind her back.

"No! He's not getting it. Don't forget what happened to Julie Sloane. It might have been him that took her."

"Do you swear on your mother's life?" I ask him.

"I swear! I swear!"

"Take no notice, Sparra, he was gonna put the handcuffs on us yesterday."

"But he just swore on his mother's life!"

"Well, make him swear on his Dad's life as well," says Debbie.

"I swear, honest to God, on me mother's and father's life, just give me the radio!"

Debbie takes it from behind her back and holds it out. He tries to move his arm out to get it but he can't reach.

"Make the sign of the cross! Cos that means you die if you tell a lie!" says Debbie.

He moves his hand and makes a sign of the cross, it's not a very good one cos he can't move his hands very far, but Debbie gives him the radio anyway. He takes it in his hand and tries to put it to his ear, but his arm moves really slowly and when he puts it by his ear he looks like he's going to cry. He brings it down from his ear and gives it a little shake. He does everything really slowly and groans every time he moves.

"Do you think he'll be able to fix it then, Debbie?"

"I don't know, maybe, probably."

"What if he does?"

"All the other coppers will come running down here to help him and then they'll come and get us, so we better get going now."

"No! Don't go. Get help, please! Jesus Christ, you're not leaving me."

Debbie starts to go towards the ladder.

"You'll be OK, the other coppers will come and get you."

"They won't. They don't know I'm here."

"Well fix the radio then."

We start climbing up the ladder.

"Come back here now you little bastards or else! When I get out of here you pair of shites are gonna be in more trouble than you can even dream of . . ."

Debbie stops climbing.

"See Sparra, me Dad's right, that Sniffer, he's just a pig like all the rest. I told you we have to watch our backs."

Sniffer drops the radio.

"Who are you calling a pig? Little fuckin' bastards."

CHAPTER
NINE

I don't want to think about him any more cos I don't know what to do. I'm going to think about the street party instead, so the first thing I do when I get home is look in the cupboard under the stairs. I pull out the biscuit tin where we always keep the fireworks and open it. It's empty! What's going on? Me Dad always gets them in for the street party.

"Mam! Mam!" I shout up the stairs.

"Rebecca, hold on, I'll be down in a minute."

But I can't wait, so I run straight up and into her room. She's bending down putting something in the wardrobe. I can't see what it is cos it's all wrapped up in a paper bag. She turns round quickly when she sees me and shuts the wardrobe door.

"Rebecca! I said wait downstairs, didn't I?"

Her voice is kind of blurry, like it is when her and me Dad go to the pub together and come home talking all happy and daft.

"Mam, we've got no fireworks. Is me Dad gonna bring some in?"

She looks at me funny and says, "No love, he's not. He's got to work the late shift."

"But Mam, has he got to work the late shift all the time? He must have to come home sometimes. What about his clean clothes? He can't stay in work with the same clothes on all the time."

She looks over at the chest of drawers where me Dad keeps his clothes. I see where she's looking and I run over and pull out all the drawers one by one. They're all empty! Nothing in them except for some old brown paper and fluff.

"All me Dad's clothes are gone! Where are they? When is he coming back?"

"He'll be back soon love, don't you worry. His clothes are in the Baggy."

But I don't think his clothes are all in the Baggy cos you don't leave them there. You have to stay by the machine and wait till they're washed and then take them home and hang them in the yard. Unless you're rich, cos rich people put them in the dryer, but even they have to wait for the machines to finish so they can take the clothes home again.

"But Mam, his clothes can't be still in the Baggy."

Mam turns around, picks up a blouse from the bed and starts to fold it.

"The machine got stuck and I had to leave them there till the man comes to fix it."

"When's the man coming to fix it?"

She shakes the blouse she just folded and starts to fold it again, even though she already had it done.

"They're on strike today so I don't know."

I don't know what to think. If me Dad's clothes are all stuck in a machine in the Baggy, what's he going wear? Mam puts her arm around me and gives me a little squashy hug.

"Tell you what love, come downstairs and I'll give you some money to go the chippy."

I love going the chippy and I love chips, so I run down the stairs and grab her purse. She comes down really slow and nearly trips over when she gets to the bottom, but it's not a funny trip over cos she's got tears in her eyes. I better not ask her any more questions cos it seems to make her cry. I hate it when me Mam cries. Mams aren't supposed to cry.

"Be careful now, just go the chippy and come straight back. No messing. Do you hear me?"

"Yes Mam."

She sits down in front of the telly and starts watching the news. She never watches the news. I think she's going to get up in a minute and switch over but she doesn't. I think she's been hypnotized. I saw that on the telly once. A hypnotist came on and he talked and talked to this woman in a dead-soft, slow voice. He kept telling her to relax until she fell asleep. Then he told her that when she woke up she was gonna be a really good singer and that she'd be in a big concert.

As soon as the woman woke up she started singing in a really stupid voice. She thought she sounded great and kept getting louder and louder even though she sounded like a big, rusty nail being scraped down a blackboard. Everyone laughed and her husband came on and said she was usually very shy. When everyone stopped laughing, the hypnotist clicked his fingers and the woman changed back to her ordinary self. She nearly went mental when he told her she'd been singing and making a holy show of herself all over the place. Maybe that's what happened to Mam. I hope not. I like her the way she always is, just ordinary and having lots of tea and biccies all day. Not all blurry and tripping up.

"Mam, do you want me to turn over and see if there's a game show on?"

"If you like, love," she says, still sitting staring at the news.

But before I get to the telly a policeman's face comes up. He looks a bit like Shelby, really annoyed and lots of wrinkles. He says that a young police constable has gone missing in Liverpool. They're very worried about him and anyone who knows anything has to ring a special number.

That must be Sniffer-cop! Unless there's another one gone missing. Maybe there is, they didn't say anything about him having a cold so maybe it's not him. The special number to ring has got two sevens and a three, or is it a four, no I think there's a three and then there was a five. Oh God I've forgotten already. I want to remember it but I can't cos they said it really quick. I want to call in to Debbie's to see if she saw it and maybe she remembered the numbers, cos she's good at numbers and I'm not unless someone helps me. But I can't call in cos I have to be really good like me Mam said and go straight to the chippy.

There's a great big queue outside. I could have gone up the road to the other chippy, there's never a queue outside that one but that's cos the chips are horrible, all stuck together in a heap and squashed like someone sat on them. Anyway, I don't mind queuing outside Billy's chippy cos there's always something to see and there's a lovely smell: chips, fish and vinegar.

All the people in the queue are standing close together, trying not to look as though they're going to push each other out of the way to get in the door. There's a dog barking and it's coming from the lamp-post just outside the chippy. It's Stabber's dog and he's sitting down, looking fierce. Some kid runs up to him and throws him a chip and the dog licks it for a bit, then gobbles it up. His mouth's like a big suction thingy and it stays open like he's ready to get more chips.

Stabber must be in the chippy getting his dinner. He must be running short of dead bodies and his brother's sausages. Rosie the chip-woman goes really fast and before I know it I'm down as far as the door. Stabber's dog is looking at me. Debbie says Alsatian dogs can bite your whole arm off in one go and kill you in two seconds exactly. This is the closest I've ever been to one but I don't mind cos he's tied to the lamp-post and he can't get me. He doesn't really look all that fierce from here. He's got sad eyes that follow you all around no matter what way you go. He looks a bit lonely and I can't resist reaching over and giving him a little tiny pat on the head. He doesn't bite me or growl, just holds up his paw, like he wants to shake hands. I take his paw in me hand, it feels nice and soft, though the black bits underneath are a bit rough and I wouldn't fancy getting scraped with his claws, they're really long and sharp.

Just then, Stabber comes walking out of the chippy with a big bag of chips under his arm. I let go of the dog's paw real quick and turn me head towards the wall. I'm not quick enough though cos he taps me on the shoulder and when I turn round there he is smiling at me. Good job there's loads of people in the queue, otherwise he'd get me and turn me into a pudding to have after his chips. "Are you all right then?" he asks.

I stick me lips together. He gives me a funny look, then goes and unties his dog. The two of them walk down the road and Stabber's doing his funny walk with his arm stuck out.

I stand inside the door out of the cold. Good job too cos I can see two dirty great big coppers coming towards the chippy. Rosie looks up at me. She's got yellow hair and a greasy squashed-up nose. She's on her own today, trying to get all the chips cooked and wrapped to stop everyone in the queue moaning about her. Her husband Billy's supposed to be there, but everyone knows he's a plonkie and whenever he goes on the ale he leaves poor Rosie to do the chips all by herself. She's got no kids either. I heard me Mam saying she had it out, all of it. That means her stomach's completely empty apart from her dinner!

I like Rosie though cos she's always nice to me and always gives me a couple of someone else's chips to eat when I'm waiting for mine. As soon as she sees me she gives me a wink. "Hello, love," she says. But before I can answer the two big coppers come walking in the door. I hide behind the man in front of me so they can't see me.

"We're calling in to ask if anyone knows anything about the policeman that's gone missing," says the biggest, oldest copper.

Everyone ignores him.

"All we're asking is if anyone knows anything, anything at all, that they come forward and tell us," says the other one.

"We're very worried, he could be hurt or injured," says the first one.

"No such bleedin' luck," says a man with hairy sideburns. His mates all laugh.

"Oi! Who said that?" shouts the biggest copper.

A woman in the queue says, "I didn't hear anything did you, Peggy?"

The Peggy-woman says, "Nah Doreen, I didn't hear a thing."

Then Peggy starts shouting up and down the queue, "Did anyone hear anything?" Lots of people shake their heads, then Peggy and Doreen start asking each other if they heard anything and then they start shaking their heads from side to side. The man with the sideburns and his mates start doing it as well and they all start laughing. The two policemen aren't laughing though, and the old one looks like he's gonna go bonkers.

"This is a very serious matter and if you lot don't . . ." But he doesn't get to finish off what he's saying cos Peggy butts in and says, "Hey! Can anyone smell pork?" They crack up laughing even more and the man with the sideburns and his mates start going "Oink, oink, oink." Peggy and Doreen join in and so do a few more people, they make a little circle, all going "Oink, oink, oink!"

Everyone else in the queue just stares at the counter and one man keeps counting his money over and over again. The two coppers go red and walk out of the shop really fast. Peggy runs to the door and shouts, "Go on, fuck off back to woolly-back land!" and then runs back in.

Rosie picks up her little chip shovel and starts banging it on the counter. Everyone goes quiet and looks at her.

"Haven't you lot got any shame? That copper that's missing's got a mother and father just like the rest of us . . ."

Doreen butts in, "Speak for yourself, love."

Rosie bangs her little shovel again. "What's wrong with everyone? I think it's terrible, that's only a bit of a lad that's missing, he's only twenty-one and anything could have happened to him. He's a human being you know."

"Since when have pigs been human?" shouts Peggy.

Rosie puts her eyebrows so high up they're nearly touching her hair. She starts to stare at me and says, "For Christ sake that's no way to carry on in front of kids."

"What would you know about kids, Rosie?"

Rosie just shakes her head. She looks at me again and says, "Right love, what do you want?"

"Two fish cakes and two bags of chips please," I say.

"Hey Rosie, we were before her," says Peggy.

"Well this is my shop and I'll serve who the hell I like, when I like, and if you don't like it you can piss off up the road and get your chips there."

Everyone goes quiet then and Rosie grabs me hand and puts six chips on it for me to eat while I'm waiting. They're hot and I have to throw them from one hand to the other to stop them burning. The queue's dead quiet and Rosie turns her back and starts shovelling the chips again. It's my turn now and she hands me the chips and fish cakes all wrapped up in white paper and the pink football page from the *Echo*.

When I get home me Mam hasn't even warmed the plates and the kettle's not on. She's still sitting staring at the telly. There's a programme on about some old people who eat dry bread and cat food and only have a candle cos they can't afford the electric.

"I got the chips, Mam."

"Good girl, love."

That's all she says. She doesn't even get the plates. I go into the kitchen and I get the plates, the knives, the forks and two glasses of milk.

I bring it all in to the living room cos it doesn't look like me Mam's gonna come in the kitchen. I watch her eat her chips. Even when she's putting chips in her mouth she doesn't come out of her trance. She's like one of them Daleks from *Doctor Who*. The chips are lovely and crunchy but she doesn't even smile. When we've finished I lean against her, but she doesn't put her arm round me. I think she's being horrible. I went the chippy all by myself and I came straight back like I was supposed to and she still just sits there. She's dead mean!

I jump up and go into the kitchen, open all the cupboard doors and bang them shut. I listen for her to start shouting but she doesn't. I bang all the doors again and again and I keep banging them until me arms are nearly hanging off. Still nothing, she still doesn't shout. She must be hypnotized. She usually hates me banging doors and making noise. If she hadn't been hypnotized she would have shouted at me. I run back into the living room and just as I do the doorbell rings. It must be me Dad! He must have forgotten his key. I run to the door and open it but it's not me Dad, it's Auntie Mo. She doesn't even say hello to me. She just pushes me out of the way and barges in. She goes straight to me Mam and sits beside her on the couch, right where I was sitting.

"Are you all right, Karen?" she says.

"Me Mam won't do anything. She keeps sitting there and she won't do nothing!"

I wish I'd kept me mouth shut, cos now I've gone and given that Mo an excuse to shout at me again.

"Oh shut your face, you! I'm trying to talk to your mother. Go and wash yourself, you look filthy as usual."

"I'm not filthy."

"Don't answer back. Go and wash yourself before I take a scrubbing brush to you."

"But I want to stay here with me Mam."

Before I can say anything else she jumps up and runs at me. She belts me right across the face with the back of her hand and it really stings. No one ever hit me in the face before. Mam looks at me and looks at Mo. Her mouth's open like she's going to say something. I'm waiting for her to save me, but she doesn't. She's just sitting there and she's letting Mo be the boss of the house. Then Mo says, "Get upstairs, you! Go on, you've caused enough trouble!"

I run up to me room. I know I'm going to cry cos me eyes are shuddering and so's me lip. I don't want that Mo to see me cry, she'd be made up.

She shouts up the stairs, "You stay up there till I say so."

I go to the window and look out. All the kids have brought the wood and stacked it up in the middle of the road to make a bonfire. It's not fair, why should I be stuck up here when it's the street party? I take me shoes off, put them under me arm and tiptoe down the stairs, then I hunch down and sneak through the kitchen and out the back door. Auntie Mo's big screechy voice is going on and on so I know they can't hear me. I run down the back entry and come out in the middle of the street. I look up to see if anyone's looking out of our house, but no one is. I run to Debbie's and knock on the door. She opens the door, peeps out at me, then runs back inside and comes back with a bag. She puts her finger on her lips.

"Ssh. Mam's gone the bingo, me Dad's asleep, let's get going before he wakes up," she says.

We keep quiet until we get round the corner.

"All the coppers are looking for Sniffer. They were on telly and in the chippy," I tell her.

"I know, I know. I saw it on the telly."

"Did you hear the special number?"

"No, me Dad turned over to the cartoons."

"The coppers in the chippy were asking everyone to tell them where he is."

"You didn't tell them anything did you?"

"Course not, it's our secret."

"Swear?"

"I swear and I cross me heart and hope to die." I make a cross on me heart and so does Debbie. Then she looks around to see if anyone's there and nudges me.

"Look what I've got!"

She opens her bag and takes out her torch. I know what she's got that for.

CHAPTER
TEN

"I want to go back to the Bommy," says Debbie.

"No, we should stay away."

"It was our special place till that Sniffer came along. Anyway I was thinking about it. He can't move, can he? And if he can't move he can't get us, can he? Come on Sparra. Don't be chicken, he can't do nothing."

I hate being chicken. I want to be good. Mind you, I was good and me Mam didn't even notice and she let that Mo slap me in the face, for nothing. I just wanted to stay with me Mam but she cares more about that Mo than she does about me, and Mo's never good, not ever.

"OK, but let's just stay a few minutes."

"Yeah, we will. Guess what else I've got?" She opens her bag again and takes out a bottle.

"It's wine. It's been in the back of our cupboard for ages."

"Won't your Mam and Dad go mad?"

"They've forgotten about it cos they don't like it. Go on, taste it, I've already had some."

She passes it to me.

I take a swig and it's not a bit nice, I thought it would be like Dandelion and Burdock.

"I think it's gone rotten, Debbie. We better not drink it."

"No, it's meant to taste horrible. Me Dad always gives me some of his brown ale, it's horrible as well but he says you have to get used to it, so's you'll be ready for when you get big and can have loads. Here, have another go."

So I take another mouthful. It's still not nice. Someone opens a door behind us, so I have to stick the bottle down me jumper and we run off. When we get to the main road I stop. Debbie doesn't want to wait and she grabs me and shouts, "Look left, look right, look left again," and pulls me by the arm through the traffic. All the horns are honking at us, but Debbie keeps laughing and pulling me all over the place. The cars are swerving and nearly banging into each other but we don't care.

"Let's do zigzag," says Debbie.

"Yeah, come on."

So we go zigzag all sideways and there's a big lorry coming and he has to go sideways as well, then he stops and beeps his horn, so then we zigzag the other way and a black taxi comes along and has to go sideways like the lorry. When we get to the pavement we can't stop laughing cos all the cars have stopped and everyone's shouting out of their car windows and beeping their horns.

When we get to the Bommy, Debbie goes down the ladder first. It's really dark. It smells different, worse than when the mattress was here.

"Come on Sparra, come down and see Sniffer for a sec."

I start to climb down. Me foot slips off one of the steps. I grab the side and cling on.

"Hurry up, will you? I'm on me own down here," shouts Debbie.

Sniffer makes a coughing noise. Debbie shines the torch on him. I stop climbing and look at him. The light is on his face, it's really white and his eyes are looking up at me. I can feel the goose pimples coming up on the back of me arms. When I get down I stand right beside Debbie, there's a wet puddle around Sniffer's legs. I can feel me heart banging. Sniffer's eyes are really only half open, so even though he's staring at us, it's like he can only see our bottom halves.

"Help me, get someone," he says. His voice has gone kind of small and whispery, I think there's something stuck in his throat cos he's making funny noises as well.

"Help me. Help me," he says.

"Maybe we could give him a drink of your wine, Debbie."

"No! That's for us."

"Just a little bit."

"No, the minute we go near him he'll grab us."

"He must be dead thirsty, Debbie. Maybe we should give him a little sip. You watch his hands so he can't grab me."

Sniffer tries to hold his head up but it kind of falls back down. "Help," he whispers.

Debbie takes a sip of wine. "He never even said please. Hey you Sniffer, listen to me, you have to say please if you want something." His eyes look wet and one of them blinks. A tear runs away down the side of his cheek.

"Please, please, please, please," he whispers. Debbie passes me the wine and I bend down to give him a sip. Suddenly I feel his hand on mine, it feels cold and wet. The smell of wee goes right up me nose. I snatch me hand away real quick and jump up. Debbie hops around, pointing her finger at Sniffer.

"See! See! What did I tell you? He was gonna grab you and murder you. Well he's not getting a friggin' drink now." She grabs the wine and takes a big gulp and I do the same. I feel a bit dizzy, like when we're playing run round in circles, only I haven't been running around. Debbie grabs the bottle and takes another big gulp, but she's got too much in her mouth and two dribbles come out each side and fall down her chin.

"Hey Debbie, you look like Dracula! Let's play Dracula running round in circles." I take a big gulp and open me mouth. It starts dribbling out, now we both can be Dracula. We start to run round and round Sniffer in a circle. Both of us start flapping our arms up and down. We're going faster and faster and faster and every time we go round Sniffer he tilts his head back and looks up at us. He makes moaning noises but we take no notice of him, cos now we know that if we try to help him he'll try and grab us. We keep going and going. I think if we go fast enough the wind will take us up in the air and we'll be able to fly around like proper Draculas but all of a sudden me head goes spinning and me knees just sort of fold up. I land on the floor with me head right beside Sniffer's head. I can smell his breath and feel his hair. I try to get up but all I can do is roll away cos the walls of the cellar start coming towards me.

"Debbie, Debbie, I can't get up. Give me a pull will you?"

She's sitting in the corner with her hands on her knees. "I don't half feel sick, do you?" she asks.

Then she opens her mouth and lots of sick comes flying out. It's coming out so fast some of it shoots out on to the wall. It's wine-sick. Not like ordinary sick cos it's red like blood. I go over to her but it seems to take me ages cos the floor is moving. I try not to look at all that red sick on the floor but I see it running down the wall and next thing I know it comes squirting out of me as well and it keeps coming until there's none left.

Debbie's head is in her lap and I think she's gone asleep.

Sniffer's whispering, "Help me, please, help . . ."

I lie down beside Debbie and then I can't hear him any more.

I must have had a little sleep cos I don't really remember anything that happened after that. It's OK though, cos Debbie's still here asleep beside me. I don't think a whole load of pork chops were really dancing round the cellar going "Oink, oink, oink," so I must have had a horrible dream. I give Debbie a shake to wake her up and she sits up really fast, just like Dracula.

"I don't feel well," she says.

I feel horrible too but I grab her by the arm and make her stand up. "Come on, we have to go. I don't know how late it is, we'll have to go home."

Sniffer's lying there being really quiet. Debbie goes over to him and pokes him with the torch in his arm, but he doesn't move. She shines the torch all over him.

"He's not moving, Sparra!"

"You're not shining the torch right, hold it still."

But even though the light is wobbling I can see his chest. It's not moving. He's not making a sound. We both kneel down so we can watch to see if he even moves a tiny bit. He doesn't. His eyes are still half open though and he's staring at us.

"It's OK, his eyes are open, if he was dead his eyes would be shut," says Debbie.

"That's right." I lean forward and look right into his eyes. He looks right back at me.

Debbie sees it too and we jump up and run to the corner. Me legs are shaking. Debbie's bottom lip is sucked right in and she's holding on to me sleeve. Sniffer hasn't moved in ages. I know his eyes are open, but what if Debbie's wrong?

Debbie's still holding me sleeve. I can smell wine from her and I can feel her feet moving. I look down and see her feet are moving from side to side, they're stuck in the pile of bandages and she's trying to get them off. All of a sudden I know what to do.

"Come on Debbie, we have to bandage him up."

"What for?"

"Cos if we bandage him up he'll be OK when the other coppers come and find him."

"But Sparra, that won't make him OK."

"Yes it will, listen to me. He'll be a Mummy! Just like in the museum. He'll live for ever! Once we make him into a Mummy he'll be all right!"

We start winding the bandages round him, quick as we can but that's not very fast. It's hard to get the bandages straight cos we keep changing our minds about which bit of him to do next. His top half is the hardest cos it's dead heavy and every time we wind the bandages round we have to move him a bit. His legs are heavy and yucky cos they're wet, and stinky too, and it's really hard to get the bandage round the one that's sticking out. We leave his head till last. Neither of us wants to touch his face, not with his eyes staring at us all the time. We have to do it though. He won't be a real Mummy if we don't, so we do it as quick as we can and try not to look until his staring eyes are covered.

Sniffer looks better when he's a Mummy, all nice and quiet. I bet he's smiling underneath. His hands are tucked in and he won't be able to try and grab us.

"Come on, let's go now," says Debbie.

"Don't forget your wine."

I pick up the bottle and hold it out to Debbie, but she doesn't take it.

"No, leave it here. I don't want to take it home in case me Mam or Dad catch me with it."

I put it on the little brick table, but Debbie shakes her head.

"No, not there, leave it in the corner where he can't reach it, we don't want the greedy pig drinking it all on us, do we?"

90

CHAPTER
ELEVEN

On the way home we keep having to stop and hold on to the windowsills cos our heads are dizzy. By the time we get to our street we feel a bit better. The party is still going. The bonfire's lit and everyone's standing around it. They're all drinking and laughing. Debbie's Mam and Dad are standing by the bonfire and they're singing a song. When they see Debbie they just wave and keep on singing, so we know she's not in trouble. There's loads of people round the fire. It's huge and the flames are jumping up all over the place. This fire is as big as last year's and that one was so big the fire brigade had to come and put it out. The police came as well and some lads threw stones at them and the next day the man on the radio said there'd been a riot in our street. The man on the radio's a dirty liar cos it was only a few stones and they were only little ones too.

I don't want to go in yet cos I don't want that Mo to get me. Me and Debbie sit on the edge of the pavement and watch the fire. There's loads and loads of sparks and one of them flies into Debbie's hair, but it's OK cos it just goes out and turns into a little piece of ash. The rest of the sparks just fly away into the air, like little bats on fire. There's lots of people on the other side of the bonfire, but it's dark and the shadows are dancing up and down, so sometimes we can see someone's nose, then an eye, just bits of faces. I'm dead tired and I shut me eyes for a second.

I open them just in time, cos the next thing is Debbie's nudging me and Uffo's there standing in front of us.

"Listen Sparra, did you tell anyone what our Lippo did?"

"No I never." I feel the short bit at the front of me hair.

"Did you tell anyone, Debbie?"

"No, not yet, but I'm gonna tell me Dad though."

"I didn't mean him to do that, honest to God. I did try and stop him," says Uffo.

He did too, maybe Uffo's not so bad. He's definitely not as bad as Lippo.

"I wanna make friends."

"You don't really, you just don't want us to tell on your Lippo," says Debbie.

"No, well I don't, but I don't want to fight any more either."

"Well who else are we gonna fight with then?"

"I dunno, what about that Terry lad from the next street? He's a bigger dickhead than me. Why don't you fight with him?"

"Terry with the red hair?" says Debbie.

"Yeah, the lad with the carrot top."

"We don't fight with anyone that's got red hair," I say.

"No, we don't," says Debbie, swinging her red plaits.

"Well what about that Griff from up the road? He's a little Nigel, he's dead brainy. His Mam said to me Mam that he's going to pass the eleven-plus and go to grammar school and he can't cos he's only ten, same as me."

"I hate little Nigels," says Debbie.

"Yeah, so do I."

I do too cos they think they're good and I hate people who think they're good and I never liked that Griff. He's definitely a little Nigel if he's going to grammar.

"Well go on then, you can fight with Griff instead of me."

"All right then Uffo, we won't fight with you no more then," says Debbie, "but I'll have to tell me Dad on your Lippo cos he cut Sparra's hair."

"No don't tell your Dad, cos they'll only fight and they're both on probation. You don't want your Dad going to prison, do you?"

"What's this about prison? Who's going to prison?" It's Auntie Mo and she's got a right gob on. Uffo runs away.

"Right Debbie, you get home and you Rebecca, can come with me. Right now, this minute!" Debbie takes ages to get up off the pavement. She keeps falling back down. "What's the matter with her?" screams Mo. "Has she been drinking?"

She yanks Debbie to her feet and sniffs her. "Jesus Christ! She's been drinking! Where's your mother, Debbie?"

Debbie's Mam must have heard and she comes over. "Get your fucking hands off my kid," she says to Mo. Mo's face nearly falls off cos Debbie's Mam's twice as big as her and she's pointing her finger right into her face and that always comes before a fight. Mo starts to say something, then changes her mind and grabs me by the shoulder and pulls me to me feet. She drags me up the street.

"Go on then, fuck off home, midget," shouts Debbie's Mam, laughing her head off.

Mo walks really quick and when we get to our house, she pushes me inside. Me Mam's standing just inside the door and she catches me before I fall over. "Leave her alone Mo, she's home now."

"Are you off your head, Karen? Can't you see the state of her? She's been drinking with that red-haired one from down the street. What do you let her hang around with her for? The father's always in trouble with the law and as for that mother! She's a bleedin' disgrace! She'd slice you up as soon as look at you. Hard as nails she is! And as for this one," she says, poking me in the cheek.

"I said leave her alone will you? You shouldn't have hit her before, you'd no right."

"What? Someone had to! Don't think I didn't notice you'd been on the bleedin' vodka when I got here. You're a right one, no wonder Brian went off. He was never any good, he's not a real man, not a proper man! Mind you, it's no wonder he's done a runner, I mean look at the state of you."

Mam shouldn't let Mo call her names and say things about me Dad like that. I love me Dad and me Mam does too. I know she does, they only fight when Mo's been around. They hardly ever fight the rest of the time. Mo keeps going on and on, saying terrible things, it's like once her mouth is open she can't stop. Her face looks like it's tied up in a knot. Mam's face is worse, though. Her eyes are nearly falling out. I've never seen her like this before.

"Yes Mo, you're right. I did have a few, but you can lay off because it won't happen again."

"See! See! I was right."

"I've just said you were right, so shut up and go home Mo. I want to put our Rebecca to bed."

"I won't shut up. Someone's got to say what's what, now me Mam's not here to say it. She used to say you had no sense and she was right."

"Well, I'm getting sense now," says me Mam and she pushes Mo towards the door.

"You can't put me out. I'm your sister. I'm your big sister."

"Then why don't you just try acting like one for a change?"

"I am, that's what I'm doing, that's why I'm telling you things straight."

"You know what, Mo? You might think you're telling things straight, but you're not. You're so busy looking for bad in everyone that you wouldn't know what straight was if it jumped up and bit you on the nose."

Then Mam pushes Mo out into the street and bangs the door behind her.

Mam sits me on the couch and looks at me, really looks at me. The hypnotism must have worn off.

"What have you been doing? You're in a right state."

"I was just playing out by the bonfire. I'm sorry Mam, I know I shouldn't have gone out but Auntie Mo was here and she hates me."

"Have you been drinking?"

I don't answer.

"I said, have you been drinking?"

I just nod.

"Where did you get it?"

"I found it by the bonfire, someone left their bottle down and I just had a little sip."

I know that's a lie, but it's only a little lie. A fib. I don't want to get Debbie into trouble with me Mam.

"Are you sure that's all you did?"

I nod again.

"Well don't ever, ever, ever do that again. Promise me, Rebecca."

"I won't, I promise. But Mam . . ."

"What?"

"You're not taking any notice of me and I had to do me own hair for school and I can't do it myself. You let Mo hit me, really hard as well. What's the matter? Why don't you like me any more?"

"I do Rebecca, course I do, don't be daft. I just . . ."

Then she stops talking and starts staring at me hair.

"What in the name of Jesus happened to your hair?"

"It got accidentally cut."

"What do you mean accidentally cut?" I put me head down and before I know it I'm crying.

"Oh come here," she gives me a hug. "I love you loads. I was upset, that's all. I'll fix your hair up lovely, don't you worry."

"Are you upset cos me Dad's gone?"

"Yes love I am, but don't you worry, he'll come back. We just had a fight that's all. Everyone does it. We just have to make up again."

"But you said he was working extra shifts and you said all his clothes got stuck in the machine in the Baggy."

"I know I did love, I didn't want you getting all bothered. He'll be home soon, so don't you worry."

"Listen Mam . . ." But she picks me up and takes me into the kitchen. Any time I try and talk she puts her fingers on me lips to make me quiet. She washes me hair and even puts some of her special lemony-rinse in to make it shiny. She takes ages brushing it and when she's finished, every single knot and tangle is gone. Then she puts me to bed and reads me my story about Emma and her magic horse and doesn't stop till the whole book is read.

When I wake up me head hurts. There's no school today cos it's Saturday.

I want to stay in bed and have a lie in, but me Mam comes up and tells me to get up.

"Do I have to? I've got a sore head. I want to stay in bed."

"You can't stay in bed, we're going to the fair today. Come here." She puts her hand on me forehead. "No temperature, I think you'll live. Is it very sore?"

It is really sore but I want to go to the fair. I love the fair, so I tell her it's just a little bit sore. We go down the stairs and she gives me half a tablet and makes me swallow it with milk.

"Now you sit there for a bit till the tablet's gone down, while I go and get ready."

She goes up to her room. I know she's going to put lipstick on. Sometimes she puts a bit on me but not when we're going out. The radio's on and it's playing happy songs. I sing along while I'm waiting cos I love singing. I can hear me Mam moving around upstairs. She's probably looking for a pair of tights with no ladders. It takes ages for her to do that cos she has to put her hands inside every single pair and move them up and down. She goes mad when she finds a ladder cos tights are dear. I hear her at the top of the stairs and then the radio stops playing nice songs and a man's voice goes: "And now for today's headlines. Concern is growing for the missing constable. There's been no sighting of him and it is feared that he may have been . . ."

"Come on you, are you ready?" Me Mam comes down and I can't hear the rest of what the man is saying. I wonder if he was going to say the special number, the one with the seven and the two threes. I wish Sniffer's mates would hurry up and find him so we can have our hidey-hole back to ourselves again. I wonder what they'll think of the bandages. They might be really pleased cos no one else round here would have bothered. The people in the chippy would have just gone "Oink, oink, oink."

The fair is right at the front of Sefton Park. Sefton Park is huge and it's got loads of things like a lake with a bandstand in it, a whole house made of glass, and lots and lots of massive big trees nearly up to the sky. The first place we go is the toffee apple stand. Me Mam gets us one each. We go straight past the Dodgems, I knew we wouldn't go on them cos me Mam hates the way they all bang into each other. If me Dad was there he'd take me on them, still I don't mind cos we're going on the Big Dipper and I love the Big Dipper. As soon as we get on, it starts moving, slowly at first but then it goes up really high and down really fast and sometimes we're on the top and sometimes we're on the bottom. We have to hang on really tight, cos if we don't we might fall out and it's so high up that if we fell we'd be all squashed into tiny little bits and they wouldn't be able to put us back together again.

Me and me Mam are laughing when we get off cos we're both dizzy. I'm made up cos I know she's not hypnotized any more. We turn round to go and find something else to go on and there's a great big copper standing there, right in front of us. He looks just like Sniffer.

I can't believe it! He must have come to get me! He's going to take me down the station and murder me! I start pulling on me Mam's hand to run away but she won't let go. Sniffer's standing there holding a bracelet and he says, "I think you've dropped something." It's Mam's bracelet. She must have dropped it when we got off the Big Dipper. She smiles at him and puts it back on. I keep pulling on her hand but she just holds on even tighter.

"Stop it Rebecca," she says and then smiles up at Sniffer. I put me hand in front of me face and try to hide but he's not even looking at me, he's staring at me Mam. He lifts his helmet up and down and then I see that his hair is lighter than Sniffer's, and it's curly, so it can't be him. Thank God! I thought I'd had it!

The copper goes away to find people to handcuff and we go to the rifle range. Me Dad's great at winning things on the rifles, that's how we got poor old Flipper. If me Dad was here now he'd get another Flipper. Me Mam's looking at the rifles like she wants to have a go, but I don't want her doing it cos she never does, only me Dad goes on the rifles.

"Come on Rebecca, let's have a go on this," she says, dragging me closer.

"No, I don't want to."

"Oh come on, it'll be a laugh."

"No."

The man at the rifle range has seen us and he's got a big stupid grin on his face and he's calling me Mam over.

"Well you wait there then. I'll have a go myself," she says, looking at the man and putting on a wiggly walk to make him look at her some more. Me Dad hates it when she does that. He says she does it on purpose to make men look at her. I think he's right cos she doesn't walk like that in our house. She picks up the rifle and shoots. I can't believe it, the bullet goes straight into the red bit in the middle and the next one and the next one.

"You've got a goldfish love, come and look at them and see which one you want," says the man, winking at me Mam. She goes to the goldfish. There's a lovely goldy one in the middle, it's dead shiny but Mam doesn't even look at that one, she points to one that's more red than gold, not a bit like Flipper. I go running over. "Can I pick it, can I pick it, can I pick it, can I pick it, please, please, please!"

"I think she wants to pick it love," says the man, winking again.

"Go on then Rebecca, you pick one." They're both laughing at me, I can tell. I hate it when grown-ups do that: look at you and laugh as if they know a secret and you don't.

I pick the lovely shiny goldy one and the man takes it off the shelf and hands it to me. "Now love, whatever you do, don't forget to give him his steak and onions when you get in," and then he winks again. I can't stand the way he winks, his eyes are so ugly he should wink with both of them, then nobody would have to look at the ugly beady things any more.

"Fish don't eat steak and onions. Everyone knows fish eat fish food."

"She's a clever kid that one," says the man.

"She gets it off me," says me Mam.

On the way out of the fair we get candy floss so we can eat it walking along the road. Mam eats hers really quick, but I've still got loads, all big and pink and sticky. I like to make it last a long, long time. One time I made it last for hours and hours.

We stop at the pet shop. The parrot's gone. Someone must have bought it. I hope they got a big cage for him. We go inside. It smells like fish food, bird seeds and parrot poo all mixed up. Mam buys a lovely glass bowl for our new Flipper and on the way home she carries it in both hands, really carefully, so's it doesn't fall and smash into a million bits like the other one. Me candy floss is so big that I can hardly see anything when we're walking up our street, and it's still big when we get to the door. Flipper never stops swimming all the way home, round and round his plastic bag.

Mam can't open the door cos she's holding the bowl, and she puts it on the step while she gets her keys out. While she's looking in her bag I sit on the step and put the plastic bag in the bowl, so Flipper can get a good look at his new house before I empty him in. He must really like it cos he swims even faster. Me Mam opens the door and I'm just about to stand up when I see four dark shoes and four dark legs. I look up the legs and see more dark: dark jackets and dark helmets. It's the two coppers from the chippy and they're right by our step. They look really annoyed and I know they've come to get me. One of them is staring at me and the other one looks at me Mam. He says, "We'd like to ask you a few questions," and taps his jacket pocket. I can hear a metal sound. Handcuffs!

CHAPTER
TWELVE

I start running. I can hear me Mam shouting, "Come back! Oh my God!" I don't care what she says. I heard the handcuffs and I'm not coming back! I'm running down the middle of the street and I'm going so fast that I only hear the screeching noise of the car when it's really, really close. I turn around and it swerves off the road and goes up on the pavement. I can see a copper as well. He's running after me. All the doors in our street are shut, if there was one open I could run inside and hide behind their couch. The copper'd never think of looking there and they'd never find me. I'm getting near the entry. I'll run up there and into the next street and then maybe someone'll have the door open and I can find somewhere to hide. I can't half run fast. I'm the fastest runner in our school. I can run faster than the boys. I get into the entry, but it's full of bins and they're all blocking the way. I have to go zigzag all around them and it's dead hard to run fast when you have to go zigzag. The copper's right behind me now. There's dog poo all over the place and I've gone and run on top of some. I can feel it all squelchy on me shoes. Oh God! Me Mam'll kill me cos they're me good shoes as well. Someone's left a battered old chair outside their back door and I run straight into it. All of a sudden there's something on me shoulder, it's a great big hand. He's got me! I try and run but he holds on to me, so tight all I can do is run on the spot. Then me Mam comes running into the entry.

"Rebecca, for Christ sake what's wrong with you?"

"He's trying to put handcuffs on me! Don't let him Mam!"

"What? What handcuffs?"

Mam looks at the copper but he smiles at her and shrugs his shoulders.

Me Mam takes me hand and the copper lets go. Mam holds me really tight.

"For crying out loud, Rebecca, you could have been killed on the road. What in God's name did you do that for?"

"Mam! Mam! Listen! He was gonna put handcuffs on me and take me away! He was Mam! Honest to God!"

The copper puts a big innocent face on and holds his empty hands out to me Mam to make a liar out of me.

"They're in his pocket, he's hiding them from you!"

But Mam just looks at me like I've got two heads and the copper keeps on smiling.

"Come on, take her home, sometimes kids are afraid of us, I think it's the helmets," he says, touching his hat.

"She never usually does anything like this. I don't know what got into her," says me Mam, holding me hand dead tight while we all walk back up the street. When we get inside, both the coppers come in and sit on our couch. Me Mam puts me sitting on a cushion on the floor and I can see under their chins and the old one's got lots of little black dots under his.

"What's your name, love?" says the younger one.

I'm not saying nothing cos if they know me name they might put me in jail.

"Rebecca," says me Mam. I give her a dirty look but she just shakes her head.

"Rebecca, you've nothing to be frightened of. We're not going to do anything to you, we just wanted to talk to your Mum, that's all," he says.

I'm still not saying nothing cos I know he's telling lies. Now me Mam has gone and told him me name as well. She shouldn't have told him anything. She's smiling at him as well and now he's smiling at her. They've gone and fooled her. Any minute now and they'll stick the handcuffs on the two of us. Then she'll believe me.

The old one's horrible, there's a big warty thing on his nose and he must be really ancient cos his wrinkles are everywhere, even on his neck. He keeps looking all around at our living room, like he wants to make sure he sees every single thing. He's staring at Flipper now. Me Mam put him on the floor in the bowl and I think that old copper's after him. He probably wants to take him away. Debbie says sometimes coppers come marching into her house and take things away. They don't even knock on the door. Well, they're not getting my Flipper and they're not getting me.

"Thanks for catching her, I was dead scared she'd get hit by a car," says me Mam.

"It was lucky she didn't. You have to watch out when you cross the road, Rebecca. Didn't they teach you that in school?" says the young copper, squidging his eyes at me.

"What school do you go to then?"

He just wants to know so he can come and get me when me Mam's not there. Well I'm not telling him and that's that.

"Would you like a nice cup of tea?" says me Mam. "You must be thirsty after all that running."

"Yes please," says the young one.

"No thanks," says the old warty one and gives the young one a dirty look.

"I think I'll leave it thanks, we can't stay long," says the young one. He's got a hooky nose, kind of turned up at the end.

"Are you sure? It's no bother," says me Mam, looking at Hooky-Nose. He's going to answer cos he opens his mouth but old Warty butts in, with a big gob on him.

"Quite sure. Now I'm Sergeant Woods and this is Constable Stanley, you've probably heard on the news that one of our officers has gone missing in this area."

"I've heard about it on the radio," says me Mam.

"We're calling on every house in the area to see if anyone has heard or seen anything that might help us find him."

"I don't know anything."

"Have you heard any gossip about him?"

"No, I haven't."

"Have you seen anyone acting out of the ordinary or any strange goings-on?"

"No, like I said, I haven't seen or heard anything."

Old Warty gets a nasty look on his face and takes a picture out of his pocket and shows it to me Mam.

"Have you ever seen him before?"

I can't see the picture, only the back. Mam looks at it and shakes her head.

"Really? Well, he's been on the beat here for months. You must have seen him walking around. He must have gone up and down this street hundreds of times."

"No, I haven't seen him, they all look the same to me," says me Mam. "I mean with the uniforms and hats and . . ."

"Have another look, Miss." He puts the picture real close to me Mam's face and taps it. Mam's face goes red.

"I'm not 'Miss', I'm married."

Warty looks around our living room again and he puts a nasty smirk on his face.

"If you say so," he says, looking at the young copper and grinning.

"What are you on about? Are you trying to say I'm lying about being married?"

"Look love, there's loads of women on the game round here, we know the score. We're not here to talk about that, so don't worry, just take another look at the picture and see if you can help us, that's all we're here for."

"On the game? What are you talking about? You're saying you think I'm on the game! Jesus Christ! The cheek of you! In front of my kid as well."

Me Mam's really annoyed cos I think the copper's trying to say that she just plays games all day. That's not fair cos me Mam does loads of things. She keeps our house dead clean. She does the windows every week and she washes the step every single day. Then when she's done all that she makes our dinner and sometimes she makes a pudding as well.

"Now look here, don't get snotty with me. I'm getting sick and tired of you people. There's a young officer, a good man too, gone missing and so far not one person in the whole area can tell us a single thing. Someone must know something," says Warty.

"Well, no wonder no one wants to talk to you when you talk to us like that! How would you like someone saying something like that to your wife?"

"My wife's a respectable married woman!"

"Well so am I."

She keeps looking at Hooky-Nose. It's like she's waiting for him to say something. He just keeps eating his lip.

"Proud of your mate are you?" says me Mam. He just looks at her. Warty hands her the photo. She takes it by the corner and holds it out.

"Just look at the picture and see if you can remember anything."

"Like I said, I don't know anything and I've never seen him before. If I did I would have told you before," says me Mam and slaps the picture back into his hand. She's gone even more red.

Warty looks at me. "What about you? Do you know anything?"

"For Christ sake! She's not even ten yet. What would she know about missing policemen?"

Me Mam's sticking up for me, she's not going to let him take me away. But old Warty keeps giving me funny looks.

"If you ask me, it's pretty strange for a little kid to run away just because there's policemen at the door."

Hooky-Nose looks at Warty and he puts both of his hands on his knees.

"Maybe she was just scared because of something she saw on the television, you know, one of those crime shows."

"Yeah they've all got televisions, these people," says Warty.

"What do you mean by 'these people'?" says me Mam.

"You know exactly what I mean."

"No I don't. I must be thick mustn't I? Since I live round here."

The young policeman starts to cough. "Er, I think what Sergeant Woods means is that we're very worried about our missing colleague. He's been gone days now and there hasn't been any sightings, none at all. We're hoping that somebody knows something, even kids might have seen something, heard something . . ."

He's trying to fool me Mam again, to get her to tell him things, but she's still all red and she's not smiling at all now.

"Oh so now you're trying to say kids might have done it. What exactly do you think the kids might have done? Maybe they put a gun to his head and drove him off in a van. Is that it? Or wait, I know, I bet they tied him up and buried him in the park. Maybe he got beaten up by a nine year old! You two make me laugh, coming round here like this. I used to stick up for you lot when people said you were all a waste of space, well I won't any more. Why don't you get out there and look for him instead of coming in here and accusing us of all sorts?"

"I'm sorry, we have to ask questions, it's our job. Nothing personal, you understand."

"Well there's nothing wrong with your job but there's something wrong with the way you're doing it . . . nothing personal, you understand."

"Look would you . . .?"

"Go on. I've answered your questions. Now get out of my house and go and catch some criminals. And while you're at it why don't you pick up a few kerb-crawlers. They're up and down these streets every day! Can't you see them? Or is it OK cos it's not your street they're driving up and down? It's not your wife they're saying dirty things to and it's not your kids they're following around?"

"We do our best, Ma'am," says Hooky-Nose.

"Harassing women and frightening little kids! If that's your best you know where you can stick it!"

Warty stands up and folds his arms. He laughs, but it's not a funny laugh, cos his mouth is pointing down.

"Oh here we go. Harassing you now are we? Typical, all we do is come and ask a few questions and they start accusing us of harassment. You wouldn't know what harassment was, love, and believe me, you wouldn't want to find out!"

"What? What are you on about? Is that a threat?" Mam stands up and she looks like she's going to cry. Hooky-Nose stands up and puts his hand on her arm.

"Look don't get upset, that's not what he meant."

"Get your hands off me," says me Mam, pulling her arm away.

"Sorry, I was just trying . . ."

"Well don't try anything else, just go before I call the, call the . . ." Mam looks around like she's looking for something she's lost.

"Yeah love, who are you gonna call? Oh and what exactly are you going to use to call them on? You haven't even got a phone," says Warty.

"Get out of my house now!" Mam shouts.

"Come on, I told you we were wasting our time with these people. They're all the same, they all stick together like flies on shite!"

Warty goes out the door and Hooky-Nose is about to follow him when he stops and says, "Look I'm sorry for disturbing you. Thank you for your time, if you hear anything would you let us know?"

He's still trying to be nice but it doesn't work cos me Mam just gives him a dirty look and the second he gets outside, she bangs the door behind them. She doesn't

111

say anything but I know me Mam's really annoyed with them and I feel better cos she stuck up for me.

"Mam, you won't let them take me away, will you?"

"Of course not. They'll never take you away and they're not coming into this house ever again either, not after that, so don't you worry." She goes into the kitchen. I know she's going to put the kettle on and make a nice cup of tea cos those men were horrible to her and a nice cup of tea always cheers her up. Me Mam's only been in the kitchen a second when I hear a strange noise behind me. Somebody's tapping on the window. I jump up to see who it is. When I get to the window there's nobody there, but then somebody starts knocking on our front door.

CHAPTER
THIRTEEN

I hope it's not the coppers back again. I go to the door and peep out. It's Josie! I love Josie! She's me Mam's bezzie mate and Mam always smiles when Josie comes round cos she says dead funny things and makes us laugh. She always says you have to laugh, even when things go wrong. Me Mam comes running back in and looks through the window, she's frowning cos she probably thinks it's the coppers back again as well. When she sees who it is she runs to the door and opens it, smiling before she's even got there.

Josie's got her hair done black. Last time I saw her it was bright yellow. She always says a change is as good as a rest. She looks lovely, just like someone off the telly. She's got lovely big dangly earrings and they're like two Oxo cubes. She's got a lovely handbag shaped like a packet of Smarties and it's got bendy handles on it. She gets new handbags all the time, cos she likes to be in fashion. I love her handbags, especially when she opens them cos she always, always takes something nice out and gives it to me. Last time she gave me a clip-on earring. It's real pearl and it's worth a fortune. She said she lost the other one when she was dancing. It's dead shiny and it's the loveliest one I've ever seen. I only wear it for best.

They go into the kitchen and I follow. Josie gives me Mam a brown paper bag. I can easy guess what it is cos it's cake-shaped. Josie always brings cake. She puts her arm round me Mam's shoulder.

"Are you all right, love?" she asks.

But me Mam doesn't answer, she looks at me and Josie nods. They've got that kind of face on that grown-ups get when they want to get shut of you so they can talk about secrets. Josie opens her handbag and hands me some money.

"Here love, you go run to the shop and get me ten ciggies and get yourself some sweets with the change."

She puts loads of money in me hand. I don't know how much the ciggies are but I bet there'll be loads left for sweets. I don't go to Mister Abdul's shop because he never sells ciggies to kids even if they are for their Mam or Dad, so I run down the shop on the main road.

The woman in the shop says, "Are these for your Dad, ducks?" I nod and she gives me the ciggies. When I tell her I want to buy Mojos with the change, she goes, "Do you know you'll get eighty-eight Mojos with all this change?"

"Will I? That's great!" I say.

She gets a right gob on then, cos she has to count them all. She gets as far as thirty-nine when this old man comes into the shop and shouts, "Gis the *Echo* love." She loses her place and she has to start again, it takes her ages. When she's finished she puts them all in a white paper bag and twists the top. Mojos are me favourite cos even when you're finished eating them you're not really finished cos there's always some left, stuck to the back of your teeth. You can leave it there for ages and that way you can have some later if you want.

When I get in Josie's cutting the cake. It's her favourite one, Battenburg. It's got lovely pink and white squares on the inside and on the outside it's yellow and the yellow comes off and you can suck it. We all sit down and eat it.

"You're getting big. What have you been eating?" asks Josie.

"Chips and mash and chicken stew and Mojos."

"No wonder. I hope you're doing well in school. I bet you're giving those teachers lip, just like me and your Mam used to," she says, grinning. I look at me Mam to see if she's grinning, but she's not.

"No Josie, I'm dead good in school and I got a gold star for me sums."

"A gold star! You must be a genius, we never got any gold stars."

"They didn't have any gold stars when we went to school, Josie," says me Mam.

"Well even if they did, we wouldn't have got them, that's for sure," says Josie.

They both laugh and Mam says, "I think they would have given you a gold star for some things."

"Hey, not in front of the kid. That reminds me, I brought something for you. Do you want a pressie?"

"Yes please, yes please."

She fiddles in her bag and takes out a little plastic thing. She opens the lid and it's got all green stuff in it.

"What is it?"

"It's eye-shadow, what do you think?"

"It's gorgeous."

"You can have it. I'm only wearing blue now."

Me Mam looks at it and says, "Only for dressing up in the house, not for outside."

Josie takes out her compact. It's got a mirror and a little round woolly thing in it and she puts lots of powder on her face with it. When she's powdery enough she blows a kiss at herself in the mirror.

"Come on Karen, let's go out for a drink. It'll be like the old days," she says.

"I can't. I've got no one to mind Rebecca."

Josie puts her compact down and grabs me hand. She swings it round and round.

"You'll be fine on your own for an hour, won't you love?"

"Yeah, I'll be good."

"See? She'll be OK."

"No, she's far too young and the cops were here today asking all sorts of questions about the one that's missing. They might come back."

"No they won't. I saw loads of them going down Upper Parliament Street. They won't come back around this way again, not for ages anyway."

"No! God knows what she'd get up to."

"Don't be soft. Look at her. She's a big girl now. She can look after herself for an hour. We were on our own when we were much younger than your Rebecca."

"I know, but it was different then."

"Yeah, it was much worse. Oh you worry too much, Karen. Come on, you need a good laugh."

"I'll be all right Mam, I promise I'll be dead good. Honest to God."

She's not sure now. I think she really wants to go out but she can't make up her mind. I've never been on me own in the house before, but I don't mind. I can watch whatever I want on the telly.

"Come on Karen, it's bright outside, she'll be fine. Won't you Rebecca?"

"I will. I will. I promise I will."

Me Mam stands up and I know she's going to say yes.

"Will you promise not to answer the door and stay here till we get back Rebecca?"

"I promise I promise. Cross me heart and hope to die."

"OK then. We won't be long and when I come back I'll bring you a packet of crisps."

"Can I have cheese and onion?"

"Yes, but only if you're good and don't wreck the place the minute me back's turned and don't go outside the front door. Not even one foot, do you hear me?"

Josie starts laughing. "And not even your little toe, do you hear me?"

"And if anyone knocks don't answer, pretend you're not here."

"I won't answer the door, I double-treble promise."

Mam runs upstairs to get ready. Josie sits by me on the couch and starts telling me this big long story about her boss in the material shop where she works. Her boss is called Mister Smedders and he always uses six big long words when all he needs is one little one. Josie's always copying him to make us laugh and whenever she does she sits up real straight, then puts her lips all to one side.

"This is not Woolworth's Josephine, this is a high-class-high-quality-materials-and-sewing-requirement-retail-outlet. Please remove that stuff what's on your face and conduct yourself accordingly. Our assistants must be nice girls at all times Josephine, none of that common stuff." Josie always snorts when she copies him cos she says that's what he does. Whenever Mister Smedders turns his back she always sticks her tongue out and pretends to pick her nose with her little finger and flicks imaginary crows at him. She says she never gets caught doing it cos she's not soft and every time he turns round she just folds her arms and smiles like an angel. One day I went to her shop with me Mam to get a zip for me Dad's good trousers and Josie was there and the first thing she did was blow me a kiss. Her lips were lovely and red like a big tomato, so old Smedders mustn't have made her wash it off that day. When me Mam gave her the money for the zip Josie pretended to press some buttons on the till, then she put the money back in me Mam's hand and winked at me. Smedders was in the corner fiddling with the button rack and Josie pulled a face at him and said, "Well he can afford it, can't he? Daft old bugger!"

Mam takes ages getting ready. When she comes down her hair's all done curly at the front. She must have used the tongs. She always uses them when she goes out and sometimes she does mine with them as well. She's got blue eye-shadow on, and red lipstick the same as Josie. She's got her best flared trousers on and they're so long they cover the ends of her platforms and her brown T-shirt is so tight it makes her bosoms stick out. She looks like a magazine lady.

Josie jumps off the couch when she sees me Mam. "Jesus! Karen, you look great. Doesn't she look brilliant, Rebecca?"

"She looks the best."

Mam twirls around to show her bum to Josie. "Do these trousers make me bum stick out, Josie?"

"What bum? You haven't even got a bum. Don't be soft. Come on, let's get going."

Then they go to the door. Me Mam keeps going out and coming back, saying, "Now you be careful now and remember, don't open the door for anyone OK?" She goes in and out so many times that Josie grabs her and pulls her out. I watch them going down the street from our window. They're linking arms and laughing.

I'm not scared on me own cos it's not dark. The first thing I do is go upstairs into me Mam and Dad's room for a root. I love rooting, especially in me Mam's jewellery box. I'm not allowed to touch it when she's not there. But I'm going to be really careful so she won't know. I know what's in it off by heart. There's three red bangles, a cross and chain, a yellow stone thingy attached to a string, a little silver ring with a heart on it and two pairs of silver earrings, one pair's got two little stars and the other pair's got droopy diamonds hanging down. But when I open the box there's something else in there too. It's her wedding ring and her engagement ring. She never takes them off. How did they come to be in her jewellery box? She told me that the engagement ring is for when you're going to marry someone one day and the wedding ring is for when you're married. Me Mam is married. She's married to me Dad. She said married women never take their rings off cos if they do they get bad luck. When she comes back I'm going to tell her to put them on, she must have forgotten. What if me Dad sees them? He'll go mental. I pull back a bit of lino in the corner and hide them under there. When me Dad comes back I'm going to whisper to me Mam where I hid them and she can put them on real quick so me Dad won't ever know she took them off. They're not very big. They don't make much of a bubble in the lino. A little spider comes out and runs across the floor. Everyone hates spiders, but I like them. Dad says they keep all the flies out of the house and I hate flies, they're all buzzy and they sit on dog poo. This spider must be scared, maybe he's gone looking for his Mam and Dad. He must have found them cos he disappears into a crack in the wall.

I wish I could find me Dad. Maybe he'll come home today. He hardly ever works on Saturday. I think I'll make him something to eat just in case. I made minestrone soup one time, me Mam lit the gas and opened the tin though, cos she doesn't let me play with matches. But I'm bigger now so it's OK.

I go downstairs. There's not much in the cupboards, me Mam must have forgot to go shopping. I know what I'll do. I'll make him some toffee. It will be a special treat cos he loves toffee. I've watched me Mam make it loads of times. You just get butter and sugar and stir it all up. You can put raisins in it as well. We haven't got any raisins but we've got butter and lots of sugar. I put them in the pan and mix them up. Next I strike the match and turn the gas on, but the match goes out and I have to strike loads cos they all keep going out. I hide all the used matches under the rubbish in the bin cos I'll get told off for wasting them. Loads of gas is coming out of the cooker and the kitchen smells like rotten eggs so I get the air freshener, the one that smells like roses. I spray about twenty squirts into the air. At last the gas lights and I put the pan on the cooker. The butter turns into watery stuff really quick and it's all bubbly, even though the sugar's stuck in the middle. I must have done something wrong. I know what it is, I forgot to stir it. I get a big red spoon from the drawer and start to stir it in the pan. All of a sudden the spoon feels lighter and I try to pull it out, but it's stuck! I pull and pull but only the handle comes out. The rest of it has melted and now the toffee's got red gloopy stuff all over it. It doesn't half stink. There's a black smelly cloud coming out of the pan now and it's making me eyes water and me nose itchy. I turn the gas off but the smoke still keeps on coming out and me toffee's just a big stinky mess. Then I hear the door open.

121

CHAPTER
FOURTEEN

"What the hell's going on here?"

It's me Dad! Me Dad's come home. I run to meet him and he catches me and twirls me round.

"What's that horrible smell?"

"I was making toffee for your dinner, Dad."

"Where's your Mam?"

"She's gone out with Josie."

"Are you on your own?"

"Yes and I've been really good too, I didn't go out."

He takes me by the hand and brings me into the kitchen. He looks in the pan and coughs.

"That's a plastic spoon, that's only for salad. It's melted, soft girl."

"I didn't know, Dad. I just wanted to make something nice for you."

"I know you did, sunshine, not to worry."

Then the door opens and me Mam and Josie walk in, but when Josie sees me Dad is there she turns round and says, "Oh I have to go now, I'll see you later Karen."

Me Mam is smiling cos she's really pleased to see me Dad but he's not smiling.

"What do you think you're doing leaving her on her own, Karen?"

"I only left her for half an hour."

"Yeah, well, see what she's done. She could have burned the house down."

"Dad! Dad! I didn't mean to. I didn't burn the house down."

Me Mam goes into the kitchen. She picks up the pan, puts it in the sink and turns the tap on. Then she opens the window and the back door.

"I just went down the road with Josie."

"You went off drinking with your mate and left our Rebecca here all on her own."

"Oh for God's sake, Brian. I only had half a lager-shandy. You left us on our own. What did you expect me to do?"

"Well, I didn't expect you to get all done up and start going out pubbin' and clubbin'."

"Pubbin' and clubbin'! I was only gone half an hour."

"You shouldn't have."

"Don't you come in here shouting the odds at me! Some father you are, going off when you feel like it."

"You made me! You wanted me to go."

"No Brian, you wanted to go."

"Oh there you go, that's typical of you, twisting things round."

"Why don't you just leave me alone?"

"Right then, I will."

Why can't they be nice to each other? I want me Dad to come home and everything to be the same as it was.

It's me own fault for making a mess in the kitchen, now he'll never come back.

"Dad! Dad! Don't go, I won't do it again, stay here Dad and I promise I'll just sit in the corner and read comics. I won't even talk. I won't even eat anything. I won't even do nothing."

But he won't listen, just messes me hair, gives me Mam a dirty look and walks out of the door. I want to run after him but me Mam holds on to me arm. When she lets go I run to the window and watch him going down the street. I want him to come home now. I want me Dad. Mam pulls me away from the window and says, "Get to bed you, you've done enough for one day." Then she slaps me really hard on the leg.

I pull the covers over me head. That's what I do when I'm really, really annoyed and I'm dead annoyed now. I was bad again and I didn't mean to be. How come every time I try to be good I end up being bad? All I wanted to do was make nice toffee for me Dad and now I've gone and ruined it. It wasn't my fault there was nothing in for his tea. I stay under the covers for ages until it gets dark. I'm just going asleep when I hear loud voices down in the street. Sounds like mad Harold and Skinny. I run to the window and there they are. She's in the pram this time and he's trying to push it across the road, but it's stuck. "Take the brake off, divvy," she's shouting, but Harold's looking underneath the pram and he can't find the brake. He's daft. I can see it sticking out behind the back wheel. Mad Harold keeps pushing and pushing even though anyone can see that the pram's just going to fall over. He tries to push it off the kerb and that's when it turns over and Skinny falls out. She doesn't cry or anything, just lies there on her back laughing and laughing. Her skirt's gone up and I can see her knickers as well. She doesn't care that she's making a holy show of herself and doesn't even pull her dress down. They think they're dead funny, but I don't. They're just stupid and I want to shut them up so I run to me bed and take one of me hand grenades from under me pillow. I open the window and throw it out. It hits Harold on the head and lands on the floor beside Skinny. I wish it would go bang and give them a fright, then they'd be quiet, but they just keep laughing, then Skinny picks it up and throws it at Harold. She misses and he runs after it. They think they're dead good, just cos they're on the ale, but they're not. No wonder me Dad doesn't want to live in this street no more, not when it's full of stupid people like them two. Harold pulls Skinny up and she gets back in the pram. He fastens the strap so she can't fall out again and starts pushing her up and down. A police car starts coming up the street. It's going slow and when it stops four coppers come running out. Two of them have got handcuffs dangling from their hands. They run towards Harold and he throws the hand grenade at one of them. They all run back to their car, duck down and kneel on the pavement with their hands over their faces. Another police car comes from the other end of the street. It makes screechy noises and then it starts going backwards all the way back to the end again. It just stays there and nobody gets out.

It's all gone really quiet, the four coppers are still hiding, I think they're all waiting for the hand grenade to make a big explosion. Mad Harold is pointing at it and laughing his head off, then he starts shouting at them.

"It's only a kid's toy! Are youse soft or what?"

Then one of the coppers stands up and goes towards the hand grenade. He picks it up and waves to the others, they all stand in a circle looking at it. Then the one with the hand grenade in his hand goes over to Harold and punches him right in the nose. There's all blood coming out of Harold's nose and it's dripping down his shirt.

"Hey there's no need for that, it was only a laugh, just a kid's toy," he says and he's not laughing any more.

Skinny's arms and legs are dangling down the sides of the pram and her head's going up and down. She hasn't stopped laughing, she sounds like a bunch of screaming seagulls. Then another copper runs at Harold and punches him again. Now Skinny stops laughing. Harold falls down. Skinny starts trying to get up out of the pram but she can't undo the straps. All she can do is wriggle about. Harold's on the ground and one of the coppers kicks him.

The other police car starts coming up the street again and two coppers get out. They're all standing around Harold in a circle and shouting. Some of them are shouting at each other and some of them are shouting at Harold. Then all of them start kicking him, except one. Harold keeps rolling around, and turning

126

over and over, and then he starts to crawl away. The copper that's not kicking Harold keeps shouting, "Stop it! Stop it!" But nobody takes any notice of him and he starts rubbing the top of his head with his hand and running around them trying to pull them off. It's Hooky-Nose, the one that came to our house. One of the others is sitting on Harold's back, trying to stop him crawling away. Hooky-Nose pulls him off and Harold starts crawling again. He gets into the middle of the road, but he must have got tired cos he's crawling slower and slower. Hooky-Nose is holding the copper that was sitting on him, but the others run into the road. One of them kicks Harold in the head and all of a sudden Harold's not crawling any more. Loads of people have opened their doors and they're all looking and shouting. A man comes running up the street, he stops halfway up. I can't see him properly but I know his voice. He starts jumping up and down and waving his fist in the air.

"Bastards! Pigs! Fuckin' Pigs! Come down here and try that on me! Come on, I'll have the whole fuckin' lot of you! You fuckin' shit-houses!"

Two of the coppers turn round and start walking towards him. The man turns and runs. I know they won't catch him cos nobody can run as fast as Debbie's Dad.

The two coppers turn back, laughing. The one that kicked Harold pushes him with his foot so Harold's lying on his face, he pulls his arms real hard and puts the handcuffs on him. Then three of them drag him to the police car, open the back door and push him in.

Skinny is screaming and screaming but they just laugh at her cos she's still stuck in the pram.

Nosy Noreen comes out, even though everyone can see she's got rollers in her hair, they're all sticking out of her hairnet. She lives opposite us and she's always looking out of the window. Me Dad says she doesn't miss a trick. She starts shouting.

"Hey you lot! I saw that! You can't do that, that's police brutality that is!"

But the copper with me hand grenade turns round and goes right up to her. He sticks his face in real close to hers and he shouts at her, "Resisting arrest, you fucking old slag, and if you don't shut the fuck up Missus, you'll get the fucking same!" She runs in and shuts the door, but I can see her curtains moving and I know she's still watching when the police cars drive away, just like me.

Me Mam comes running up the stairs, she must have been watching too. I run and hide under the covers so when she comes in she thinks I'm asleep. She just stands in the doorway for a minute then goes away again. I can't go asleep cos I can't stop listening out in case the coppers come back again. Then I hear a knock on the door so I run to the window. It's Josie back again and she's got a big bag in her hand. I think she might have pressies and I really want to go and see her but I don't go downstairs cos I don't want to get slapped again. Me Mam wouldn't have slapped me if her and me Dad hadn't had a row. She would have known I didn't mean to melt the spoon. They used to always laugh when I accidentally did something wrong. Like last year when I made a snowman in the back yard. It took me ages to pile all the snow up with me little shovel and when I'd finished I gave him potato eyes and a carrot mouth. It was the best snowman in the street. Except he didn't last long cos I'd put all the snow against the back door, so it wouldn't open and I couldn't get back in the house! Mam and Dad weren't a bit annoyed when they heard me banging on the door and saw what I'd done. They thought it was funny and helped me make another one in the corner of the yard. Now everything's gone horrible, as horrible as could be.

Even our street's gone all wrong, wrong, wrong! Everyone's gonna go mad, cos Harold got battered. Even though they all think he's a bit soft in the head, they all like him really, cos in the daytime he's dead friendly and he always says "Hello, howdo?" And everyone always grins and answers back, "I'm fine Harold. How's the head?"

Skinny'll miss him. I wonder what she'll do now. She'll have nobody to push in their pram cos as well as her baby going away to Heaven, her Harold will never ever come back now, not ever. I don't think she's going to be laughing any more.

Maybe if I hadn't thrown the hand grenade Harold might not have got battered. But then I don't know. Maybe they would have got him anyway. Maybe they were looking for someone to batter. Maybe they were looking for somebody to put the handcuffs on. Maybe they were looking for me.

CHAPTER
FIFTEEN

I woke up loads of times last night cos I dreamed the coppers were coming to get me and kick me the way they kicked Harold. But every time I woke up I heard me Mam and Josie talking, so I know it was just bad dreams again. I used to dream of really nice things like toffee apples and me and Debbie having adventures but now all I dream is horrible things, horrible nasty coppers in helmets coming to get me with great big pairs of handcuffs.

When I go downstairs me Mam and Josie are asleep on the couch and there's bottles of ale on the floor. All their blue eye-shadow is messed up and they don't look so nice, not like they did yesterday. There's nothing to eat. Not even any bread. Then I see the Battenburg cake, so I have some of that.

Josie calls me so I go back into the living room. She's rubbing her eyes so hard that her eyelashes fall off and stick to her cheek. It looks like a spider is crawling on her face. She picks them off with two long red nails and puts them in her handbag.

"Jesus! These are supposed to stay on. I paid a fortune for them," she says, licking her lips and trying to fix her sticky-up hair.

"Why did you stay in our house last night, Josie?"

"Just to keep your Mam company, love." She pats me Mam on the shoulder, but she's fast asleep and takes no notice.

"What's wrong with her?"

"Nothing a nice cup of tea won't sort out. You go and put the kettle on, there's a love."

"But me Mam'll kill me if I go near the gas."

"Go on love, she's asleep. I won't tell her."

"But she might wake up and I've got to be good or me Dad won't come back."

"Oh come 'ere." She puts her arms out and I go and sit on her knee even though I'm too big. She gives me a cuddle and whispers in me ear.

"Your Dad will come back, don't you worry. They love each other but they've had a fight like the way daft old grown-ups do and it's nothing to do with you. It's not your fault grown-ups fight, love."

"But I've done something really terrible."

"No you haven't."

"I have . . ."

She puts her finger on me lips.

"All you did was burn a spoon and that was just an accident, you're not bad, you're very good. Now come on and we'll make some tea. I'm spitting feathers."

Josie walks into the kitchen with her hand on her head. She fills the kettle, puts it on the cooker and lights the gas. She points out of the window and I look out to see the pan I burnt. Mam must have put it outside in the back yard in case it burnt the house down. I feel bad cos that was me Mam's good pan, but Josie is smiling at me.

"I'll buy your Mam another pan, don't you fret. Worse things happen at sea."

"Like what? What happens at sea?"

"Oh it's just a joke, love. God that kettle's taking ages to boil, I can't wait."

Then she turns the tap on and puts her mouth under it. She sticks her lips around the tap and starts slurping the water down. When she's finished she wipes her mouth with her sleeve. She laughs at me cos I'm looking at her a bit funny.

"Don't you pick up me bad habits, will you? Your mother'd skin me alive if she saw me."

"I won't and I won't tell on you either."

"Good, we can have a secret just for us. Sometimes it's good to have a secret."

"I've got another secret, Josie."

But me Mam wakes up and calls Josie and she puts her finger on me lips again.

"Shh. Listen love, you go out and play for a bit and I'll give the place a good tidy up and when you come back your Mam'll be awake and then we can all go to New Brighton."

I love New Brighton. "Can we go now? Can we go now?"

"No not yet. Tell you what, make sure you don't get into any mischief and don't stay out too long and then we can go this afternoon."

I run out the back door before she changes her mind. I'm going to call for Debbie. Nobody answers for ages until at last her littlest brother comes to the door. He's got lemon curd and toast on his face. They always have that for breakfast in their house. He's only wearing the top half of his pyjamas. That's cos he always wets them, so his Mam doesn't bother putting the bottom half on him.

"Are oo looking for our Deb?" He talks in baby talk, cos he's the baby of the house even though he's four and big enough to talk proper.

"Yeah, where is she?"

"She's gone de baggie-waggie."

I run up the road and I'm there in no time cos it's not far. There's loads of baggies round here but there's only one open on a Sunday so I know which one she'll be in. It doesn't look like a proper baggie. It looks like a house except for the wire stuff on the windows. I look in to see if Debbie's there. I don't really want to go in unless she's definitely there. It's full of cranky women all shouting at each other and grinning at their smelly babies while they wait for their machines to stop. The floor is always wet and there's soap powder stuck all over it. It smells horrible as well, like dirty washing and old wee. I can see Debbie down the back, so I go in. She's sitting on the edge of the wooden bench, holding on tight to the handle of her washing-wheeler. She hasn't put on her washing yet cos all the machines are full.

"Hiya, Sparra."

"Hiya, Debbie. Are you waiting for that machine?"

She's staring at an old lady who's pulling her washing out of the machine.

"Yeah, I've been waiting ages and ages but it's my turn now."

The old lady takes her clothes out really slowly and folds them all up as if they were really nice and not all scruffy and raggy. She's got a string bag tied round her hand and I can see a tin of cat food inside it. I bet she's one of those old ladies off the telly and she's gonna have cat food for dinner. She takes out this big long yellow cardie, it's all full of holes but she still folds it and strokes it like a cat. Debbie starts giggling so I do too. The old lady turns round and she shakes her fist and goes "Tut tut." She's got long grey whiskers on her chin. Debbie says that old ladies turn into men when they get old. One of our bin men has got big bosoms like a lady, so I think men turn into women as well. I don't ever ever want to get old. I want to stay a girl.

The old lady puts all her clothes in a big black plastic bag and she walks really slowly to the door. It takes her ages and by the time the old lady's gone, Debbie's got all her washing in the machine.

"Hey you," says a big fat woman.

"What?" says Debbie.

"You know quite well I was next for a machine."

"No you wasn't. I was here before you," says Debbie. I know she's trying to be brave but I think she's a bit scared cos the woman's gigantic and her teeth are all black.

"Take that washing out of that machine now or else!"

"Aah that's not fair, I was here before you," says Debbie.

"She was missus. Honest to God," I say, cos I have to stick up for me mate.

The big fat woman takes no notice of us and pulls all Debbie's washing out and throws it on the floor. I help Debbie pick it all up. We're going to be ages here now cos now we have to wait for another machine to finish. That's why I hate the baggie. When I grow up I'm going to have loads of money. I'll buy a big shiny washing machine and it'll be better than any of the ones in here.

The woman next to us stands up. She's got long red hair like Debbie's, only nearly down to her bum. She starts taking her washing out.

"Here you two, you can have this when I'm finished," she says and gives the big fat woman a dirty look, cos she must know that fat woman cheated Debbie out of her machine.

"Ta," says Debbie.

"Did you give me a dirty look?" says the big fat woman to the red-haired woman.

"So what if I did?"

"Don't you give me dirty looks, carrot-top!"

"I'll look the way I want. You shouldn't have robbed the machine off the little girls. You know quite well they were here before you."

"Aah shut your face."

"Shut your own face."

"I'll smack you one, carrot-top!"

"Just try it and I'll smack you one right back!"

The big fat woman just mumbles and goes off down the end of the shop and the red-haired woman grins at me and Debbie. "See that? That sorted her out, didn't it? You have to stick up for yourself or they'll walk all over you."

"But she was dead big," says Debbie.

"Nearly as big as Sniffer," I whisper.

"Yeah well in my book, the bigger they are, the harder they fall," says the red-haired woman. Then she puts a ciggy in her mouth and leaves it there sticking out while she takes the rest of her washing out of the machine and bundles it into a big plastic bag.

"Off you go then girls, get your washing in quick before anyone else comes and tries to take if off you."

So we shove the washing in as quick as we can, then put the powder in the drawer and the money in the slot. No one can take it now, not once it's started cos if anyone opened the door all the water would fly out and they'd be soaking wet and covered in suds. Debbie starts chewing her nails.

"Do you think that Sniffer's all right now, Sparra?" she says.

"I don't know, I hope so, I hope he's gone."

"Maybe we should go and check. See if we did the bandages right."

"We did do it right, except we didn't put any preservative on him."

"What's that?"

"Like the lotion Mams put on their faces to stop them getting old."

"Won't the bandages work then?"

"I don't know if we did them proper, like the ones in the museum."

"Come on, let's go to the museum and see. Anyway, me Mam'll only make me scrub the yard if she sees me doing nothing."

"Have you got any money?"

"It's free."

"Yeah, but the bus isn't." Debbie fiddles in her pocket but all she's got is fluff.

"We could walk."

"We don't know the way and it'd take ages and I've got to get back cos Josie's taking me to New Brighton."

"It's not fair, nobody takes me anywhere," says Debbie, sticking her lip out.

"Come on, I'll help you drag the washing-wheeler."

It's heavy now the washing's wet so we take turns. When we get to Debbie's house, I wait outside and she runs in and dumps it in the kitchen. She's in and out really quick before her Mam gets her. She has to do all the housework, just cos she's the oldest. When she comes out she's got her torch and she says, "Well, we can't go to the museum, can we? So we can go the Bommy instead."

The Bommy is just the same as it was last time, so I don't think anyone's been rooting around or anything. Sniffer's still all wrapped up in his Mummy bandages. He doesn't say anything when we shine the torch on him. Everything smells really bad, sick and wee and something even nastier, it's coming from Sniffer. The bottle of wine is in the exact same place as I put it. I pick it up and there's still loads in it, so I know old Sniffer hasn't drank any.

"Do you think we should take the bandages off him, Sparra?" says Debbie.

I go a bit closer but he smells too bad and I move back again, it goes up me nose and it feels like poison. It makes me feel sick. Debbie bends down and jumps up again quickly. She puts her hand across her nose and mouth but I can see her eyes, she's squeezing them so they're nearly shut. Then I remember something. Ages ago, there was a dead cat in the entry. He mustn't have belonged to anyone cos he lay in the corner for a week. He smelled bad and every time we went past he smelled worse and worse. One day he was gone, but you could still smell the smell for ages. It was the smell of dead! That's what Sniffer smells like. Me stomach starts to whirl around and I have to run into the corner cos now I know he's just like that cat, dead, definitely dead.

I grab the torch off Debbie but it falls on the floor. It rolls around on its own, the light moving from place to place, one second you can see Sniffer and the next you can't. One minute you can see a big bandaged head and the next you can't. I must have screamed cos Debbie starts shouting at me.

"What? What's the matter?"

I can't answer cos the words are stuck. She starts climbing up the ladder.

"No Debbie! Don't leave me on me own! Debbie! Debbie!"

She comes back down.

"I thought someone was after us, I wasn't gonna leave you but I got scared and you wouldn't say what the matter was."

"He's dead, Debbie."

"No he's not. Not properly. He's a Mummy, he can come back to life like in the museum. You said Sparra! You said!"

"No, we didn't do it right, we didn't put any preservative on him, it didn't work, the bandages have to have lotion."

"God! If the rest of them come and find him they'll kick us to bits and we'll end up like Harold," says Debbie, putting her hand over her mouth.

"I know. We can't tell anyone about Sniffer, not ever."

"No, not ever."

"What if they come round to the house and ask you about it, Debbie? What are you going to say?"

"I'm not gonna say nothing."

"Neither am I. Not even if they torture us like in the cowboy films."

"No, not even if they put our hands in the fire."

"Not even if they shoot off all our toes."

"No, not even if they pour boiling tar on our heads."

"No, me neither. Right that's it then. All we have to do is swear on holy Jesus and neither of us will ever tell."

Debbie makes the sign of the cross. "I swear on holy Jesus," she says.

"I swear on holy Jesus too."

We link our little fingers together and shake them three times. I go to pull me finger away, but Debbie keeps hers linked so I can't.

"We only tried to help him, didn't we? We didn't do nothing wrong, did we? Not on purpose?"

I think we did do something wrong, but not on purpose. It was an accident that he fell. We did try to fix his radio. We tried to ring the ambulance. Nothing worked. The other coppers won't believe we didn't do it on purpose. Sniffer didn't believe us when we said we weren't doing anything wrong. Warty didn't believe me Mam and nobody believed Harold when he said he was just having a joke. Who'd believe us?

Debbie picks up the torch and shines it on the brick table. It looks a bit like a little altar.

"Do you think Sniffer will go to Heaven?" I ask. Debbie's really good at religion. She loves hearing all the stories and she never forgets, not one little thing.

Debbie shakes her head from side to side.

"No he can't, cos he hasn't had the last prayers and the priest hasn't appointed him. I know, we can appoint him!"

"I thought a priest had to do it."

"Well, we haven't got one so we'll have to pretend. Come on, Sparra, we have to. Miss Chambers said everybody deserves the last rites, even the worst sinners."

"If we do it, do you think we'll still go to Heaven?"

"Yeah, we definitely, definitely will, cos then we've helped a sinner back on to the right path and you get let off with loads of stuff if you do that."

140

"All right Debbie, let's have a funeral."

"I'll be the priest cos I know all the holy words."

"I'll be the sad woman then, cos there has to be a sad woman crying at every funeral. What will we appoint him with?"

"We can use this," she says, picking up the wine.

Debbie always has the best ideas. I wish I'd thought of that.

She kneels down beside Sniffer, but stands up and moves away again quickly.

"He smells too bad. I'll have to throw it on him."

She throws the wine and some of it goes on his head but most of it just splashes everywhere. She puts one hand on her nose, runs towards him, empties the bottle over his head and runs back and stands beside me.

"I appoint you in the name of the Father, the Mother, the Holy Spirit and all the saints and all the others that I can't think of the names of," she says with a really holy face on. Then she joins her hands into a prayer shape and nods at me to do it as well.

"Now we have to say another prayer or he won't go to Heaven properly and he'll be waiting in Purgatroy for ages. You say Amen after I say the prayer."

"OK then."

"Right then. Now. Praise to God up in Heaven and Jesus so that they take our dearly departed into the holiest arms of the angels in Heaven. Amen."

"Amen."

"Now, you're the sad woman, so cry."

It's not much fun being a crying woman, so I only do it for a bit. Sniffer looks just the same.

"What will we do now?" asks Debbie.

"Go! Come on. I don't like it here any more."

"We'll have to find another hidey-hole."

"Not now."

"No, not next week either."

"Or the week after."

We climb up the ladder and we're just about to put the trapdoor back in its place when we hear footsteps, big footsteps.

CHAPTER
SIXTEEN

We run into the other room and crouch down on the floor. There's a hole in the wall and we have a peep through it to see who's coming. It's an old man, a very dirty scruffy old man, he's like the man in the park that time, Dirty-Face, the one that me Dad warned me about, but it's not him. This man's got a cap on and he's got longer hair, you can see lots of it coming out from underneath the cap. He's wearing loads of coats, all different lengths, and you can see the underneath ones hanging down. He's got loads of pieces of string around his neck like necklaces. He walks dead slow and we can see him looking around.

We hold our breath and don't make a sound, not even a squeak. He sits down on the floor right beside the trapdoor and takes a bottle out from under one of his coats. He opens his mouth really wide and pours it in. When it's all gone he takes a pipe out of a pocket and lights it. The smell of the pipe is horrible and I'm dying to cough but we can't or else he'll hear us. He starts banging the pipe on the floor beside the trapdoor and then he looks down.

He gets up and lights a match and starts to go down the ladder. I can hear the ladder making a noise every time he takes a step. He must have great big feet like Sniffer. I hope he doesn't fall down as well. I know when he's at the bottom cos the ladder noise stops. We hear him talking to Sniffer. "Give us a swig, mate. Go on give us a swig. Don't be tight mate, give us a swig."

We make a run for it before he comes back up and don't stop till we reach the entry in our street, then we run in and get behind the biggest bin. We're really puffed out and Debbie's face is all red.

"What do you think that tramp will do?"

"I don't know. Do you think he saw us?"

"No he didn't. I think he was dead drunk. He's a dirty tramp."

"He's a dirty plonkie."

"Yeah and if he's anything like me Dad when he gets drunk, he won't even remember, even if he did see us."

"Well then, as long as we don't tell we'll be all right then, won't we?"

We link little fingers and cross our hearts.

When we come out of the entry I can smell rice pudding everywhere. Everyone has rice pudding on a Sunday. I can see Josie sitting on the step. She blows a big puff of smoke out and waves when she sees me. She stands up and sticks her arms out, so I run till she catches me and twirls me around and around.

"What have you been up to then Rebecca?"

"Just playing and I went to the baggie with Debbie."

"Ugh that's not much fun."

"Debbie has to go every week."

"Jesus, the mother should be strung up, sending a little kid to do that. Mind you I wouldn't say that to her face though," she says, grinning.

I go up the step and am about to go into the house but Josie grabs hold of me arms and stops me.

"No Rebecca, you sit on the step for a minute while I go in and get the stuff."

"But what about me Mam?"

"Your Dad's come round and they need to be on their own so they can make up again, so your Mam's staying here and I'm going to take you to New Brighton."

"I want to see me Dad."

"You can see him later, don't worry, me and you are gonna have a great time. Now sit there and don't move and I'll be back in two ticks."

She goes in and the minute she does I go to the window. I can see me Mam and Dad in the living room. They're having a quiet fight, I can tell by their faces. They're just not shouting cos Josie's there. When Josie goes past them they don't even look at her. She goes through the living room and into the kitchen. Mam and Dad stop talking. Dad's looking at his shoes and me Mam's fidgeting with her skirt. When Josie comes out of the kitchen she's got her handbag and a shopping bag. She says something to me Mam and Dad but I can't hear what it is. I hope it's something that'll make them be friends again. I jump away from the window and sit back on the step before Josie comes out and catches me.

"Come on then Rebecca, let's get going before we miss the ferry."

"Oh we won't miss the ferry, will we?"

"No, I'm only messing, there's loads of ferries. Guess what I've got in me bag?"

"Sweets and cakes and pasties?"

"No, butties and bananas and I'm going to stop at the shop and get some nice things."

"What nice things?"

"Well ciggies for me and sweets for you."

"And Dandelion and Burdock?"

"Yeah I'll get a big bottle just for us and we'll be so fizzy our heads'll pop off."

"No they won't."

"Yes they will, cheeky. Come on, let's get a move on."

We walk to the end of our street and when we turn the corner we can see the bus coming. The bus stop is up the road a bit.

"Come on Josie, run!"

"I can't, not in these shoes."

Josie's got big platforms on. She says they're her coppin' off shoes, cos when she's wearing them nobody looks at her knock-knees.

"Tell you what, you run and tell the busman to hold on."

So I run and get to the bus stop just in time.

"Come on girl, are you getting on the bus or what?" says the bus driver. He's got a big moustache. It goes right down his chin and nearly reaches his neck.

146

"Can you wait a sec cos there's someone running. Please mister."

The driver looks out and sees Josie. She's sort of running slowly and hopping, like she's afraid of falling off her shoes.

"I don't mind waiting for her! Is she your Mam?"

I don't answer him. Me Dad always says never tell strangers nothing. So I won't.

"What's up, love? Cat got your tongue?"

I still don't answer, but Josie catches up and jumps on the bus, pulling me up by the arm. Her face is purple and she can hardly talk cos she's so puffed out.

"Where are you going my lovely?" asks the driver, grinning at her.

"Pier Head," says Josie.

He gives her the tickets and blows her a kiss. She laughs at him and we go and sit upstairs so she can smoke. I love going upstairs on the bus. You can see lots more out of the window, like houses, and flats, and more houses and flats, and when we get to town there's lots of shops. Josie doesn't look out, she's busy looking at her hands.

"Look at them. I did them this morning. Aren't they great?" she says.

Her hands are just ordinary hands, but her nails are really long and now she's got a lovely glittery blue colour on them.

"Aren't they gorgeous? It's the latest colour."

"Will you do mine like that, Josie?"

"Your Mam'd murder me. Anyway you're too young."

Josie's always all sparkly and shiny, she looks just like a holiday.

"How come you're not married, Josie?"

"I haven't met anyone with a big enough wallet yet."

"How come?"

"Cos I want to live in a posh house with a garden and then you can come and visit me and I'll have swings and a slide for you to play on. Anyway Miss Nosy Parker, I like having a laugh."

"You can still have a laugh if you get married."

But Josie just goes quiet and starts looking out of the window.

"Are we going the shop?"

"Yeah don't you worry, when we get to New Brighton the first thing we'll do is find a nice shop full of sweets and pop just for you."

When we get off the bus the driver blows more kisses at Josie, so I stick me tongue out at him.

"Hey you Rebecca, don't stick your tongue out at him, he was all right. He's got a good job on the buses."

"You wouldn't marry him would you Josie? He's got a hairy moustache."

"Beggars can't be choosers sunshine. Now move, let's get down to the ferry quick."

The ferry goes dead fast and we stand at the back to wave at the Liver Birds. All the foam pumps out like a big dragon spitting and you can smell the water, a bit like a rubbish bin but we don't mind cos it's great going fast and we love seeing all the splashes. Josie holds me hand like she's afraid I'll fall in or something. As if I would. I'm not daft. Anyway, there's loads of little spare boats on the ferry and if someone falls in the water they give them a little boat to sail in so they don't end up at the bottom of the Mersey with all the dawdlers in the sacks. There's a whole lot of seagulls following the boat. Some people throw bits of bread off the side and watch the seagulls dive for it. I don't, cos I like them better when they're flying. A boy throws a whole crust over the side and three seagulls dive for it, but the biggest seagull, one with a black mark underneath, gets there first and scoffs the crust. The three of them zoom back up like aeroplanes and then they follow us all the way from Liverpool to New Brighton, that's miles and miles and miles.

Josie always keeps her promises and the minute we get off the ferry we go the shop. She buys a bottle of Dandelion and Burdock, two packets of crisps, a big bar of chocolate for her and a little bar for me. I don't mind that she gets the big bar cos she buys me a windmill as well, it's all different colours of yellow with a roundy blue bit in the middle. It's got a long stick to hold it up in the air so the wind can make it go round and round.

"Right then, let's go on the slot machines and then we can go to the beach."

She gives me a handful of change, loads of pennies. We find the biggest arcade and go in.

"Now, you do the penny-push and I'll go over there and do the one-arm bandit. Don't wander off whatever you do, stay there till I come back or there'll be skin and hair flying!"

I put one penny in the penny-push. A bar slides forward and starts pushing the pennies. It looks like all the pennies are going to come out cos I can see lots of them are right up at the edge of the little cliff, but the sliding bar stops too soon and none of them fall.

I put another penny in, and another, still they don't fall and now I've only got one penny left. Still, I can see lots of pennies have moved and some of them are even hanging off. They have to fall down. I put me last penny in and I can hardly wait cos I'm going to be rich and I'll buy a slide and some swings and a new house with a garden. Suddenly it stops. The pennies just stay there, not one single penny falls and not one single penny comes out. I look around to see if anyone's watching, there isn't, so I give the machine a kick on the sly. There's loads of dents in it already so everyone must do it. Still nothing comes out. I bet the pennies never come out. I think the man's glued them down cos he's just a dirty swindler and wants people to put loads of pennies in so he can grab them all himself.

I go looking for Josie. I look all around the one-arm bandits but I can't see her anywhere. Where's she gone? She told me not to move, but now she's gone and moved and I don't know where she is. There's a big-eared man standing watching me. He's got a horrible grey suit with stripes and sneaky eyes. I look away and look back really quick to see if he's still watching and he is. I wish Josie would hurry up and come back before he gets me. I run towards the Fountain of Silver machine. I squash myself underneath, there's just enough room but I can hardly breathe. I can see his feet. They stand still, then one of them moves a little bit, then stays still again. After a minute the feet go away. I stay where I am cos he might come back. Then another pair of feet come along and they're platforms with purple toes. They're Josie's shoes. One of them's tapping the floor. I'm just about to climb out when back come the black shoes. They stand right beside Josie's platforms. I hope he's not going to take Josie away. I hope she takes her shoe off and gives him a good wallop. Then he says something in a big loud voice.

"Excuse me, but if you're looking for a little girl she's right here. Look, she's hiding under the Fountain of Silver."

"I might have known, come out of there Rebecca."

"No I'm not coming out."

"Come on Rebecca, don't be so daft, come out now and we can go to the beach."

"Not till he's gone away."

But she bends down and pulls me out by the arm. The man is laughing and he says, "You'd better not let that one out of your sight, she's dangerous."

They put clever grown-up grins on, then look at me and laugh. How come I'm dangerous? Me? Dangerous? He's got a stripey suit on!

The man laughs and Josie pulls me closer.

"I know, thanks for helping me, her mother would have a fit if I lost her."

"Josie! Josie! He's got a suit on!"

"You what?"

"It's stripey as well!"

"What are you on about Rebecca?"

The man grins even more at Josie. "Don't worry love. I've got one like that at home."

He walks away and Josie takes me by the hand.

"What in the name of God are you talking about? Suits? Stripey suits?"

"They come and get you in their cars Josie and then they take you away! And then there's the ones with the sacks and the ones with the hand . . ."

Suddenly I can smell ciggies and hand cream. I can't finish telling Josie cos her hand is on me mouth and I can't talk.

"Listen to me. Nobody's going to take you anywhere. I promise! And I promised your Mam I'd look after you. The only place you're going is the beach, but only if you promise to stop talking like a fruit and nut cake!"

I nod and try to think about buckets and spades and ice cream to stop myself telling the truth. I want to go to the beach and I don't want Josie to fall out with me. I love Josie even if she doesn't believe me. She can't help it really cos she's grown up and when people grow up they don't believe anything any more. I'll be like that one day. I'll forget everything that really happens and just make up new stuff and believe that instead.

"Promise me now, Rebecca, no more mad stories."

"Mm mm." I can't talk cos her hand's still on me mouth. I don't mind cos it doesn't hurt and it's nice and soft.

"OK then, be good now," she says.

She takes her hand away and smiles at me. That's why I love Josie, cos she's never really annoyed at me, she just pretends for a minute and then she always smiles and laughs and forgets she was annoyed.

"I suppose you don't want a nice big toffee-apple do you?" she says.

"I do, I do."

"Well then, what are we standing here like a pair of lemons for? Let's go and get some."

She tells the man she wants two of the biggest and tells me not to break me teeth.

We start walking down the prom to the beach and then we go down some stone steps. Josie nearly falls off cos her platforms trip her up, but I catch her and she doesn't fall. I'm made up cos sometimes when people fall they don't get up again. I don't want her to be like Sniffer. Some scruffy boys laugh at Josie and she puts her two fingers up at them and they run away. Then she goes, "Don't you ever put your fingers up like that will you, Rebecca?"

"But you did it, Josie."

"Yeah but that was by accident and I'll never do it again."

We find a lovely bit of beach. The very best bit. There's no rubbish and no wavy lines in the sand and it's not too far from the water. Josie takes a rug out of her shopping bag and puts it down. That's for us to sit on and to stop anyone else taking our bit of beach.

"Can I go for a paddle?"

She's not listening. She's looking at two men who've come and sat down near us. They're looking at her too. One of them turns round to face Josie and stretches his legs out in front of him. I can see the underneath of his shoes. There's a big hole underneath one of them. I don't know why Josie's bothered about him. He can't be rich cos it's Sunday and they must be his best shoes and if he was rich his best shoes wouldn't have holes in them. He bends forward and I can see that his mate's got greasy hair and spots.

"Josie! Josie! Can I go for a paddle?"

"OK, but just stay there, right in front of me, and don't go hiding anywhere."

I take me shoes and socks off. Josie rolls me socks into two little balls and puts one in each shoe.

The water is lovely. It's not very warm though and there's no big waves unless you count the ones I make when I start kicking the water up. I love doing that and I can get the water to go really high. It's like a big storm and I kick and I kick and I kick until I hear Josie shouting.

"Stop it, Rebecca, you'll get your clothes soaked."

I pretend not to hear her cos it's such fun kicking, but she comes running and she's running really quick as well cos she's in her bare feet. I stop kicking when she gets to me.

"I said, stop it."

"It's only water, me clothes'll dry, please can I just have one more little kick."

She looks around as if she's looking for me Mam. The man with the hole in his shoe waves at her. Then all of a sudden she starts kicking. She's making the biggest waves I've ever seen and she's laughing even though she's getting us all wet. I join in and the two of us kick loads of water everywhere. I can feel the sand underneath me feet as I kick and it feels all scratchy but I don't care cos making storms is the best, especially when Josie's here beside me making the best storm ever. We kick for ages and then Josie starts huffing and puffing and coughing.

"Come on, that's enough. I'm gasping. I need a ciggy. You can have your picnic now as well."

We're all wet and Josie's hair is all messed up. We shake ourselves and then Josie gets a towel out of the bag and gives the two of us a good rub. We sit down on our rug and she takes a ciggy out. Just when she puts it in her mouth, the man with the hole in his shoe comes over with a box of matches. He's got a big smirky grin and he says, "Light?" Josie grins back at him and holds her ciggy out towards him, even though I know she's got a box of matches in her bag.

"Ta mate," she says and she puffs on the ciggy to make sure it's lit proper, then starts rummaging in the shopping bag. She takes out some butties in a bread wrapper, then the bananas and then the chocolate and crisps. The man's still standing there and his mate's looking over and looking away and looking back again.

Josie's not taking any notice of him and she starts talking to me cos she likes me more than she likes him. Serves him right.

"Go on then love, there's your lunch, get stuck in. I bet you want the butties first before the chocolate and crisps, don't you?"

"No, I want the chocolate."

"But there's stuffed pork roll on the butties," she says, grinning and handing me the chocolate.

The chocolate's all melted and when I press it with me thumb it goes flat but I don't care cos it's lovely. Holey-Shoe is still standing there with his box of matches and he's dead jealous cos Josie's not giving him any chocolate.

"Are you having a picnic then, love?" he says to Josie.

"What's it look like? Soft lad!" she says and I'm made up cos I don't want her to marry him cos she won't get a garden and a slide and swings if she marries him.

"No need to be like that love, I was only asking," he says with a big gob on him.

"We've got some cider over there, why don't you come over and have some?"

"No ta," says Josie. "I've got a kid."

"Is she yours? We thought you were minding her or something. You haven't got a wedding ring on."

"So what?"

"Nothing." He turns round and walks back to his mate. The two of them start muttering to each other and giving us dirty looks.

Josie ignores them, picks up a big stuffed-pork-roll buttie and takes a massive bite out of the middle. Then she looks at the two men and chews her mouthful of buttie at them.

"Slag," they shout.

Josie sticks her fingers up at them.

"You said you'd never do that again, Josie."

"I know, but I forgot, love."

The two men get up and walk off and Josie laughs at them.

156

"Josie, why did they call you names?"

"Cos they're thick, that's why. That's what thick people do. They call each other names. Now come on, get yourself on the other side of that chocolate and then you can have some Dandelion and Burdock to wash it all down with."

Josie takes her little radio out of her bag and fiddles with it. Each time she does a new song comes on, or sometimes it's a screechy-sounding man talking, but she keeps fiddling until she finds a song she likes. I like this song too and I've seen it on the telly. The man that sings it has long hair. He wears gold trousers and loads of make-up. Josie starts humming along, but then all of a sudden she goes "Oh yeah!" and claps her hands as well. Josie's not like an old woman, she never goes into the shop and starts moaning about this being too dear or that being too dear. She doesn't count her change and she doesn't care about anything. Like now, lots of people are looking at her singing her head off and she just sings "Oh yeah!" and claps more and more. There's a woman sitting near us and she keeps giving Josie a dirty look and she keeps shaking her head. I can't hear her but I know she's going "Tut, tut" cos that's what old women do, they just "Tut" and "Tut" all day.

Josie notices her and she shouts over, "Well? I'm enjoying myself, aren't I?"

And the woman shakes her head and goes "Tut, tut, tut," just like I knew she would.

Josie keeps singing and singing and the woman's going mad. She's tutting and tutting louder and louder, so Josie sings louder and louder till nearly everyone on the beach is looking at her. Then she stops and looks at them all and she says, "Well? Watcha think you're all gawping at? Have I got a welly on me head or something?"

Then they all turn round and start looking at the water and the woman has one more little tut and then takes her butties out and eats them dead slow. I bet they're horrible butties. I bet she's only got margarine on them. Josie opens the crisps and starts putting them in our stuffed-pork-roll butties and gives me one. It's the nicest buttie I've ever had. Josie is the best cook. She always mixes up funny things to make them taste better. Like one time when me Mam and Dad went out and Josie was minding me, she made toast and eggs for our tea. She chopped up eggs and mashed them all up in a bowl and when she'd got them all squashed she put great big squirts of brown sauce and ketchup in and mixed it all up. Then she put it on the toast and cut the toast into lots of little triangles. It looked horrible, but it tasted lovely, like a surprise.

When we've finished our lunch we drink all the Dandelion and Burdock and Josie lies back on the rug.

"Can I make a sandcastle?"

"You haven't got a bucket and spade love."

"Can I have one, please?"

She takes out her purse and looks in it.

"Here you go, you run back up the steps and go to the stall and get yourself a bucket and spade. Come straight back now and no dawdling and no messing and . . . no hiding and if there's anything I haven't thought of, don't do that either!"

"I promise. Thanks, Josie."

I run all the way and I get the best yellow bucket and spade on the stall. There's a picture of a little fish on the bucket. The fish is a bit like Flipper except he's longer.

When I get back Josie's making wheezy noises and her eyes are closed. I can see where one of her eyelashes is starting to come off and is sticking up. It looks like it's winking at the sun.

I love digging. The sand is soft and comes up really easy. First of all I just fill the bucket and empty it into one big pile. Then I start squashing the sand really tight into the bucket so as to make bucket shapes to go on top of the pile, so it looks like a real castle. It takes me ages and Josie has her eyes shut the whole time. She's going to get a brilliant surprise when she opens them. The last thing I do is put the windmill on top. It doesn't go round and round cos there's no wind, but it looks lovely.

When Josie opens her eyes she looks at me sandcastle and says, "Oh my God! Look at the size of that sandcastle. How long have I been asleep?"

"I don't know. Do you think me sandcastle's good?"

"I think it's the best sandcastle I've ever seen."

Then she looks at her watch and goes mad. "Oh my God! Look at the time, I must have been asleep for ages. Jesus Christ! Quick Rebecca, hurry up. We'll have to go or else your Mam'll have me guts for garters!"

I stick me lip out cos I don't want to go home, but Josie grabs it and gives it a wobble with her finger and says, "Put that lip back in you! Come on, if you're

159

quick we'll be able to get a stick of rock on the way to the ferry."

We go so fast down the road that we're nearly past all the shops.

"Josie, don't forget me stick of rock, you promised."

"God you won't stop till you've got me last penny will you, Rebecca?" she says, but she's laughing and stops at the very last shop. It's not really a shop. It's a van and it's got one side open and a big counter sticking out. Hanging off one side of the counter is a load of buckets and spades and orange balls in nets and on the other side is a rack of postcards. New Brighton doesn't look like New Brighton on the postcards. Maybe they fixed it up especially nice for the pictures.

The man behind the counter of the van has got his shirt open and he's got curly black hairs all over his big brown yucky fat belly.

"What can I do for you love?"

"A stick of rock please," says Josie and puts the money down on the counter.

"Can we have one for me to take home to Debbie too?"

I nearly forgot I promised Debbie some sweets and I've gone and eaten all the chocolate and crisps.

"Oh God! I'll have to stay in and knit every night this week."

"Please Josie."

"Oh all right then, can't say no to you, can I love?" she says and nods to the man.

The man nods his head and hands me the sticks of rock.

160

"Keep the change," says Josie.

"There isn't any," says the man.

The ferry is waiting for us and it's so full I'm scared they won't let us on. We have to push our way through lots of people to get down to the back so we can see the splashes and wave goodbye to New Brighton. When we've finished waving we sit on the wooden seats and watch the seagulls. I put me head on Josie's lap cos I feel sleepy. Josie puts her radio on and I hear a man saying, "Police are still looking for the missing constable. Sources say foul play is suspected." I wonder what foul play is? Foul is terrible like a smell and so they must mean terrible play, but only kids play. Maybe they think me and Debbie did it. Maybe the coppers will all be waiting with handcuffs when we get off the ferry. I ask Josie if we can stay on the ferry and go back to New Brighton, but she tells me to go asleep. I don't want to go asleep but there's a bit of sand in me eyes, and it's making them sore so I just shut them for a minute and the next thing is Josie's got me by the hand and is pulling me off the ferry. I get ready to run, but the only person there is the man who opens the gate. Good job too, cos Josie's holding me hand so tight I'd never get away.

It takes ages for the bus to come. Josie says it's cos it's a Sunday and half the drivers go out on the razzle on Saturday night and can't get up for work. We go upstairs again and Josie lights a ciggy. She loves to smoke, I can tell by the way she always takes a big puff and looks happy when she blows it out.

"Will me Dad still be there, Josie?"

"I hope so love, but never you mind. If he's not, he'll come back to see you soon."

"It's all cos of me Auntie Mo you know. She started it."

"I know love, but your Auntie Mo doesn't know her arse from her elbow and your Mam feels sorry for her."

"Why?"

"Cos it's not easy for her."

"Why?"

"Cos of the way she is."

"What? What do you mean?"

"Never you mind," she says and gives me ear a little pull.

"Me Dad'll stay home, won't he?"

"Course he will, me little fruit-and-nut-cake, don't you fret."

I can't stop fretting though and the more I try not to fret the more I do. When the bus gets to our stop I want to run really fast, but I can't cos Josie doesn't let go of me hand for a second. I think I'll never get back up my street to see if me Dad's there. If he's not there I don't know what I'll do. Josie's walking dead slow in her platforms. When we get halfway up our street I swing me arm to see if she'll let go but she won't, so I start twisting it round and round. After a bit she stops walking and bends down to me.

"Listen Rebecca, stop messing. I know you like to do a runner now and again but I'm not letting go of your hand until we get in the house, so stop swinging out of me."

"OK, sorry Josie."

"Not to worry, sunshine. I know you can't wait to get in."

"Will me Dad be there? Will me Dad be there?"

"Fingers crossed," she says.

CHAPTER
SEVENTEEN

Me Mam must have seen us out of the window cos the door opens the minute we get to the step. I run in past her and into the living room. There's nobody there. I go into the kitchen and there he is. Me Dad is sitting at the table drinking a cup of tea, just like he always does. I run towards him and jump on him. He stands up and swings me round and round.

"Dad! Dad! Are you staying with us now? Are you staying with us now?"

He sits back down again and puts me on his knee, he rubs his cheek on mine and I can feel his stabby whiskers. He must have forgotten to shave today. Usually he has a lovely smooth face.

"I can't love."

"Why not?"

"Cos me and your Mam's splitting up."

"But you can't split up! You're me Mam and Dad. You live here with us! In our house! In our street!"

"I know love, but sometimes it goes like that."

"I promise I'll be very good. As good as gold, Dad."

"I know you will but it's not that. It's me and your Mam that's not getting on, not you and me. I'll still be your Dad."

"Where are you going to live Dad?"

"Up the road. I'll be able to come and see you loads of times. It'll be just the same."

"It won't be the same, not if you're not here."

"I know love. Look, I'll tell you what, I promise you I'll try and make things nearly the same as they were."

"But I want everything to be exactly the same."

He rubs me cheek and kisses me on the ear but he doesn't answer me.

"Why can't you and Mam get on like you used to?"

"I think it's cos we got married too young."

That's the stupidest thing I've ever heard, cos I know they were both sixteen when they got married and that's not young. It's not like as if they were only nine or ten.

Me Mam comes into the kitchen then.

"Did you tell her?"

"I did," he says and he looks all sad.

"Things will be OK, Rebecca, you'll see."

I take no notice of her cos I hate her. She's making me Dad go away. I keep tight hold of me Dad cos I'm not going to let go, that way he'll have to stay.

"Your Dad has to go now, Rebecca, get down off his knee," says me Mam.

But I won't. I know she's going to make him go away and I'm not letting her. She takes hold of me and tries to pull me away, but I'm not letting go. She pulls me again.

"Wait a minute, will you? She'll be all right if you don't pull her," says me Dad. He stands up. I keep hold of him and can feel me legs dangling. He puts his arms around me.

"Put her down," says me Mam and she grabs hold of me arms. Me legs are swinging and I kick a cup off the table, it makes a loud crack and the handle falls off. Mam gets hold of me legs and I can feel her nails digging in. I scream and Josie comes running in.

"For God's sake! Karen, stop it!" she shouts. But Mam keeps pulling me and me Dad stands up and walks backwards but I still won't let go of him. If I can just keep hold of him a bit longer, he'll change his mind and he'll stay. I know he will.

"Karen, let go of her. Calm down, you're making it worse! Stop it!" Josie shouts.

"He has to go, Josie! He has to go! I can't stand it!"

"Jesus! Karen! He is going, just give him a chance, let him say goodbye to Rebecca for God's sake!"

But me Dad starts crying. I've never seen an old man like me Dad crying before. He must be as sad as sad can be. He's holding me so close I can hear terrible noises like he's being strangled and I can feel me hair getting wet from his tears.

"For Christ sake!" shouts Josie.

Suddenly me Mam lets go and me Dad goes backwards. He puts his hand on the wall to stop us falling over.

Mam sits down at the table and puts her hand on her forehead.

"Just go, Brian, will you? Please! I can't take it!"

Me Dad picks me up and carries me into the living room and puts me sitting on the couch.

166

"Listen love. I have to go. All this carrying on is upsetting everyone. Now you be a good girl for your Mam and I promise I'll call in tomorrow night after work."

I don't want to look at him, so I look at Flipper instead. He's just swimming around and around. He's not a bit upset, not like me, not like me Dad. Fish are stupid! Dad wipes his eyes. Me Mam comes and stands in the doorway and watches us. She's got her hand stuck in her hair, like she's going to pull some out. Me Dad looks at her then goes to the door.

"I'll be back after work to see our Rebecca, all right?"

But she just twists her hair and doesn't say anything.

"All right?" he says again.

"All right, Dad. All right Dad. All right Dad," I say, but me Mam just goes back into the kitchen and me Dad goes quietly out the door without even saying goodbye.

I stay in the living room all on me own for ages, watching stupid Flipper. I can hear noises in the kitchen, whispery noises, so I know Josie and me Mam are talking. Then I hear the tap running and plates rattling and I know somebody is putting our tea on the table. Josie comes in and takes me into the kitchen. She's got a big smile on, but it's not a proper smile, it's a pretend smile cos her eyes are still all sad.

The table is set with cups and plates and in the middle is a plate with lots of butties cut into little shapes and tiny pieces of yellow cake. I'm not hungry even though I like yellow cake.

"Come on Rebecca, eat something before you go to bed will you?" says Josie.

I don't want to eat anything and neither do they, so all the little butties and pieces of cake just end up sitting on the plate. Josie stands up and starts clearing the table.

"I'll put some tinfoil over it and you can have it tomorrow."

Mam takes no notice, so Josie gets the tinfoil and covers the plate anyway.

"Karen, do you want me to put Rebecca to bed?"

"She can put herself to bed, Josie."

"I know she can, but she's upset, Karen."

Me Mam stands up real quick and I think Josie's scared cos her mouth falls open.

But me Mam's not mad at Josie cos she doesn't scream at her to go to bed the way she does at me.

"I said I'd take her up Karen, there's no need to be like this."

"Please yourself Josie, you always do."

"What do you mean by that Karen?"

"Nothing."

"Look I know you're going through a rough time, but there's no need to take it out on me and there's no need to take it out on her either. You're me best mate and all I'm doing is trying to help you."

"I know Josie. I'm sorry, I'm cracking up."

"I know love, but you've got to think of your Rebecca. She's had a lot of upset too."

Then me Mam starts crying and she looks at me and says, "Come here love."

168

But I don't want to go over to her cos I hate her now.

"Come on love, come on," she says.

She gets up and picks me up. She starts hugging me, and I don't want to hug her back but I can't stop myself. She feels soft and warm and she smells lovely.

"I'm sorry love," she says and kisses me on the cheek. She takes me upstairs and undresses me and holds the covers back for me to get in bed.

"You're not very clean are you love? Never mind, you'll do for now, you can get washed in the morning before school."

I don't say anything, not one thing, and I'm not going to either. I'm not speaking to me Mam for ever and ever, not until she brings me Dad back and that's that!

Then she gives me more kisses, one on me forehead, one on the nose, one on each cheek and one on the chin. Then she gets Ellie from under the pillow.

"What did you do to Ellie?"

She holds him up and looks at him.

"I'll get Josie to bring me a ball of wool and knit him a nice woolly jacket next week if you like. It'd be better than tissue."

"I made him into a Mummy so he can live for ever."

"A Mummy?"

"Like we saw in the museum. Mummies can live for ever."

She smiles at me, puts Ellie on the pillow and kisses us both on the cheek.

"Night-night, sleep tight. Everything will be OK tomorrow, you'll see," she whispers. She waves three times, then goes downstairs. That's when I remember I wasn't going to talk to her ever again, but it's too late now. I've already done it.

I want to stay awake and try and hear what they're saying but I can't, they're talking too quiet and me eyes are too sore and too droopy.

I wake up when I hear the noise, a rattling noise. But it's not the milkman, it can't be, it's too dark. I hide under me blankets for a while, but I'm listening. I can't hear anything else. It's all gone quiet again. I bite me lip and a little bit comes off. I chew it and it tastes like blood. I don't mind the taste of blood. If I cut me finger I sometimes lick it clean, but I don't like to look at it though.

The rattling noise comes again, it sounds like handcuffs and I can hear voices outside our front door. I jump up, run to the window and look down. Me Mam and Josie are outside!

What are they doing out there? They've got their best clothes on. There's someone with them, a man. Mam opens the door and comes in. Then Josie follows her. The man's carrying a paper bag, it's full of bottles, I know it is cos I can hear them rattling and clinking off each other. He's coming into our house. I can't believe it, Stabber's in our house!

CHAPTER
EIGHTEEN

How did me Mam and Josie get outside? They didn't say they were going out. Maybe he kidnapped them. Maybe he's got a gun or a knife! Oh God! I have to rescue them. I've only got one hand grenade left. The coppers have got the other one. I'll just have to make do. I need things to throw but I haven't got nothing, just a box with bits of old Lego and Meccano and a doll's leg that I found in the street. That won't stop him. I have to try though. I have to rescue me Mam and Josie. Dad's not here so there's only me left to do it.

I get out of bed, really slowly so it won't creak and give the game away. Then I tiptoe across the floor and pick up me hand grenade, me Lego and Meccano. Then I get the doll's leg. I have to put that in me mouth cos me hands are full. I sneak down the stairs and am dead careful not to make a noise. I can't let him hear me. When I get to the bottom step I crouch down and stay still. I'm listening for the enemy, like the soldiers on the telly. I can hear quiet voices coming from the living room so I tiptoe towards it. When I get to the door I run in. Stabber's sitting on the couch. He looks up at me and gives me the evil eye. I want to run away and go back upstairs and hide under me bed, but he's seen me now and when he's finished killing Mam and Josie he'll run up the stairs and he'll know I'm here. I can't run away, so I start throwing me weapons. Me hand grenade gets him in the head and his mouth sort of pops open and he just looks at me. I can see his pockets, but before he reaches in them to take out his big knives I throw the Lego at him, it pings off his face and he looks really scared. He puts his hand up to his face so when I throw the Meccano it just bounces off his hand and lands on the floor.

"What in the name of God are you doing, Rebecca?" shouts me Mam.

All I have left is the doll's leg and I wait till Stabber takes his hand down before I throw it and it gets him right in the eye but he still won't surrender, all he does is rub his eye.

"Christ Almighty, what the hell are you doing? Stop it, for God's sake!"

Me Mam drags me away. Josie doesn't say anything at all. I bet she's surprised I came and rescued them, but Mam keeps shouting.

"What are you doing? What the hell did you do that for?"

"I've come to save you. I won't let Stabber take you away and kill you."

"Stabber? Who's he? What are you talking about? This is Mick. He just came in for a drink with me and Josie, that's all."

"But Mam, he kills people and takes them to his brother's shop and they chop them up with big knives and chopping things, then they make them into sausages and pork pies!"

I thought they'd be really pleased I came to save them, but Mam doesn't look pleased, not a bit. Then she says, "Rebecca, where in the name of Jesus do you get these stories? I've told you before about making things up like that."

Josie's kind of laughing and frowning at the same time. "Mick wouldn't harm a fly. Would you Mick?" She pokes Stabber in the shoulder. He just laughs.

"Mam, he's going to kill you. I know he is. Honest to God, Mam! He'll kill you for his lunch, then he'll kill Josie for his tea and then he'll kill me and I'll end up the pudding!"

They all start laughing at me. Stabber picks up a bottle of ale and takes a swig.

"Don't be stupid, he's not going to kill anyone," says Mam.

"No he's not love, of course he's not," says Josie.

Stabber looks at Josie and laughs and puts his hand on her shoulder.

"Don't let him touch you, Josie, he's just pretending. He's pretending to be nice so he can fool you."

"Nobody ever fools me, love."

But he has fooled them. Why can't they see? Just cos he's smiling. He's only doing that so's they don't watch their backs. Good job I am.

"You get out of our house! Me Dad's coming home in a minute and he'll . . ."

Mam grabs hold of me.

"Rebecca stop it, you're making a holy show of me!"

I don't care if I'm making a show of her, not even a holy show. I'd rather make a holy show than see me Mam and Josie get murdered. I wriggle and wriggle and wriggle. Then Josie stands up and comes over.

"Karen, tell you what, why don't you put the kettle on and I'll see to her."

"Honest to God Josie, I don't know what to do with her, she's going half mental. I can't cope with it," says me Mam.

"She's just got a fright that's all. Go on, put the kettle on and let me see to her."

Mam goes into the kitchen and Josie puts me sitting on her knee. Stabber gets up and stands by the door.

"You don't have to go, she didn't mean it Mick," says Josie.

"It's OK love, I have to get back and let the dog out anyway."

"OK Mick. I don't know what's the matter with her," says Josie.

"Maybe she's still upset over what happened to her the other day," says Stabber.

"What happened the other day?"

He'd better not tell. I squeeze me lips together and stare at him. "Oh nothing, probably got scared of the dog," says Stabber looking at me.

Josie pats me hair.

"Josie, I'll see you on Tuesday. Pictures and a pizza OK?"

"Ooh yeah, lovely Mick. I'll see you then."

Then he just goes out the door. He doesn't kill anyone or anything. We're saved! He's gone! I hope he never comes back.

"Pictures and . . . a pizza! Did you hear that Rebecca? Now that's a big wallet," says Josie. She looks all excited. She won't be so pleased when her toes start going missing.

Josie pats me on the head and I snuggle into her. She smells like ale and ciggies and hairspray.

"Listen to me, Rebecca. I know you got a fright, but there's no need for that. Mick's a nice fella. He wouldn't hurt you or me or your Mam."

"But Josie he's a stabber, really, really he is, he's a stabber."

"Is he now? Well tell me this, have you ever seen him stab anyone?"

"No Josie, but everyone knows he does, everyone knows."

"No they don't. It's just kids' talk. Kids make up stories and then another one adds a bit, then another one adds a bit more, then the next thing you know they all believe it."

"But it's true."

"It's not true. Do you think I'd let a murderer come into the house with me and your Mam?"

"But he fooled you, Josie, he was pretending to be nice."

"No, he *is* nice. He's lived round here for years. If he was killing people, don't you think the police would have got him and put him away?"

"Debbie's Dad says they're too busy putting good people away."

"I wouldn't take any notice of what he says love, he's three sheets to the wind himself."

"What? What do you mean?"

"Never you mind, now listen to me. Mick's a nice fella. He's not hiding anywhere, is he? He goes around the streets the same as anyone else."

"Well, maybe he's got a disguise."

"Disguise! Don't be soft! Listen Rebecca, you have to stop making up stories."

"I thought he was going to get us."

"I know you did Rebecca, but look, here we are and nothing happened. Can you see anything wrong with me? Look at me. Can you see any knife marks, any holes or any bruises?"

I can't see anything wrong with her, but that's only because I saved her before Stabber got her.

"Josie, he would have, I know he would."

"No, silly, he wouldn't. Have I ever told you a lie?"

"No, Josie."

"Well there you are. I wouldn't lie to you."

"Promise?"

"I promise."

"Cross your heart?"

"Cross me heart as well. Now you wait there a sec while I go and see if your Mam's OK."

Josie goes into the kitchen and then she comes back out with me Mam. Mam comes over and puts me on her knee.

"Listen love, we thought you were fast asleep. We just went down the road for a quick half and to get a few bottles to bring home. We bumped into Mick and we just brought him back for a laugh, that's all. There's nothing wrong with Mick. Josie likes him. Don't you, Josie?"

"He's not half bad."

"But he's got a pointy chin!"

"So what? I've got knock-knees," says Josie, laughing. Mam doesn't laugh. She looks at Josie.

"She's too young to be left on her own. God knows what'd happen. I shouldn't have went out. Don't ask me any more, cos I'm not going."

"We weren't even gone ten minutes."

"I don't care. I'm not taking any chances, from now on I'm staying in with our Rebecca and that's that!"

Josie picks up a bottle of ale and pours some into a glass. Then she drinks it all back real quick. Mam stands up and lifts me up. I wrap me legs around her middle and cling on tight. She carries me up the stairs and tucks me in. I feel funny. Like I've had two nights all in one. I don't want to dream about Stabber and I don't want to dream about me Mam and Josie hanging on hooks in Stabber's brother's butcher shop, but I know I will.

CHAPTER
NINETEEN

Mam's standing over me. She's shouting, "Get up quick, we've slept in. Get up! Get up! Come on! You're late for school and Josie's late for work."

I run downstairs. Josie is hopping around with one leg in a pair of tights and the other leg out. "Shit! Me tights are laddered. Smedders will go bonkers. Have you got any spare tights, Karen?"

"I don't know, hold on," she says and goes tearing up the stairs and forgets all about me.

I get halfway down the street when me Mam comes running after me and gives me a jam buttie to eat in me hand on the way to school. Then she goes running back to help Josie. I knock on Debbie's door but her Mam says she's already gone and she slams the door shut. I throw the jam buttie to the pigeons and run all the way to school but I know I'll never get there in time, no matter how fast I run.

Just my luck! Shelby is standing at the school gate. "Aha. You again," he says, with a big happy face on him, like he's pleased he caught me.

"Sorry I'm late, me Mam slept in, Sir."

"How old are you, Rebecca?"

"Nearly ten, Sir."

"Nearly ten, Rebecca?"

"Yes Sir, nearly ten."

"Well then, if you're nearly ten don't you think you're old enough to wake yourself up?"

"I suppose so."

"I suppose so what?"

"I suppose so, Sir."

"That's better. Now Rebecca, whose fault is it if you're late?"

"I don't know."

"You don't know?"

"No Sir, I don't know."

"Is it your mother's fault?"

"Well er . . ."

"Is it your mother's fault?"

"Only accidentally. She just forgot to get up."

"Oh, so it is her fault then?"

"No."

"No what?"

"No Sir."

"You just said she forgot to get up."

I don't know what he's going on about. I don't know what to say to him. He wants me to say something but I don't know what it is. If I knew it, I'd say it, whatever it is, cos his eyes are getting bigger and bigger and he's holding his finger out. I know what he's going to do. He pokes me in the shoulder. Miss Landers comes to the window. I can see her look out, then she goes away from the window and I can't see her. I wish she'd come out. I could ask her what to say.

"Well child?" he says, and pokes me in the other shoulder.

"What?"

Then he smacks me on the leg, really hard as well. I can feel it stinging, like I got burnt.

"Don't say what, say pardon."

"Pardon."

He holds his hand up in the air, like he's gonna smack me again.

"Say pardon Sir."

"Pardon Sir."

"That's better. Now tell me the truth. Whose fault is it you slept in?"

"I don't know. Please Sir I don't know, honest."

Wrong answer, he slaps me again, on the other leg. Now both me legs are stinging.

"I asked you to tell me the truth, Rebecca. Whose fault was it?"

"It was Stabber's fault Sir."

That's the wrong answer. I know cos he slaps me again and takes hold of me hand. He starts pulling me inside the school and when we're inside he takes me to his office, opens the door and pushes me inside.

"Hold out your hand, Rebecca."

Before I get a chance to put me hand out he grabs it and then he swings the cane back behind him. I can hear the noise it makes, a *ssshhh* as he swings it behind him and *crack* as it lands on me hand, then *tap* as it bounces off and hits the floor.

"Now, I'm asking you again and this time I want the right answer."

180

I can't answer cos me hand is really hurting me now.

"Whose fault is it you slept in?"

I've been dying to cry for ages and I've been holding me lips together to stop myself, but it's not working now and I can feel the tears coming out, there's lots of them and they're running down me cheeks and dropping on the floor. He grabs me chin and pulls me face around and the next thing I know I'm looking at a statue of Holy Mary.

"Now child, look directly into the gaze of Our Lady and pray for her to help you tell the truth."

I look at the statue but I can't think of any prayers to say so I just look at her. She's got a lovely white face with pink cheeks.

"Well, whose fault is it you were late? Answer me now child." He's still got a tight hold of me chin and keeps pointing me face at Holy Mary. When I look up I can see up his nose, two big hairy dark holes, they're opening and closing and they look like they could suck me in and I'd be stuck up there for ever. He shakes me chin and I can feel me head wobbling.

"Answer me, now!"

"Was it Holy Mary's fault?"

He goes so red I think he must be choking. Spit starts coming out his mouth and he keeps shouting and shouting, "Stupid child! Stupid child!"

He runs back and stands against the wall. He goes real quiet and then he starts smacking the end of his cane on the floor. First of all there's a quiet tapping noise, then louder, then louder still. I run towards the door, but he catches me by the arm and swings me round so hard I go flying towards the desk. I grab hold of the side to stop from falling over and then I'm trapped. He takes me hand and canes it and canes it and canes it. I keep pulling it away, so sometimes he misses, but whenever he misses he gets me the next time, only even harder. I start screaming and screaming, as loud as I can, and then the door opens.

"My God, Mister Shelby! What on earth are you doing to her? I can hear screaming down the corridor."

It's Miss Landers. She comes running in and stands in front of me.

"Mister Shelby, you're hurting her."

"Get back to your room, Miss Landers."

"I can't. I . . . I'm not."

"May I remind you, Miss Landers, that I am the headmaster here and you are the secretary? Now please go back and finish typing that letter I gave you."

He's talking kind of funny, like he's holding his breath and trying to talk at the same time.

"I won't and if you want to sack me then sack me, but I'm not leaving her here with you. I'm sick and tired of watching you hit these kids."

"Very well then, Miss Landers, consider your position here finished, as of now. And please don't ask me for a reference. Insubordination is a very serious matter."

"Do you know what Shelby? I couldn't give a shit about your fuckin' reference, so why don't you just go and shove your fuckin' job where the sun doesn't fuckin' shine?"

182

"Come on Rebecca, come with me," she says and she takes hold of me arm, nice and gentle and I go with her to her room. Shelby just stands there shaking his head and tapping his cane. I thought he might hit Miss Landers with it but he doesn't, cos he doesn't cane big people, only little people.

When we get inside her office, she shuts the door and turns the key. She puts me sitting on her special chair, the one that swivels. Miss Landers lets us sit on her swivel chair if we've been really good. She gets some tissues and wipes me eyes. I've stopped crying now even though me legs are dead sore. Me hand is too, and I can see it bleeding. Miss Landers pulls out a drawer and takes out a square box. It's the one with the Red Cross on the top. Everybody loves that box cos inside is where all the bandages and plasters and little tubes and bottles are kept and everyone loves bandages and plasters. Nobody loves the little tubes and bottles though, cos the stuff in them stings.

"Why was he hitting you, Rebecca?"

"I was late, Miss Landers."

"Ooh what a terrible crime," she says, shaking her head from side to side.

"Sorry, Miss Landers."

"Oh poor thing, I didn't mean it like that. I was being sarcas . . . well never mind, let's get you sorted out. I bet I can make you as good as new. Tell you what, you sit there for a sec and I'll go and get some hot water and a nice glass of milk. Would you like some milk, Rebecca?"

"Yes please, Miss Landers."

"How about a pink wafer?"

"Yes please, Miss Landers."

She goes out of the room and closes the door. I hear a key turning. I think she's locked me in. I hope she comes back soon. When she's gone I swivel on the chair. It goes all the way round and round. One minute I'm looking at the desk and the next minute I'm looking at the window. There's a face at the window. Shelby's face. I swivel back again. I don't want to look at him. The door handle starts to turn and I can hear someone trying to get in. I swivel round again. Shelby's not at the window any more. Someone's banging at the door and the handle is rattling like mad. I think the handle's going to break. Then it goes quiet again. I sneak a peep at the window. I can't see him. I get under the desk to hide. The door opens and I hold me breath.

"Rebecca, where are you?"

It's Miss Landers. She comes over to the desk and crouches down, then reaches in and pulls me out.

"There, come out Rebecca, you don't have to hide. I'm not going to let anyone touch you."

"But Mister Shelby is going to get me."

"No. He is not going to get you or anyone else for that matter. I'm going to call the police and tell them. He's not going to get away with this any more."

"No! Don't call the police! They'll take me away. Please, Miss Landers, don't call the police!"

"Shh. Don't you worry. He won't be here tomorrow. I promise you that."

Miss Landers' face is pink, and she must be really hot. She's got a wet forehead and under her nose I can see little drops of sweat. She doesn't wipe them though. She washes me hand and makes it all clean, then she puts lovely white bandages on. When she's finished, the bandage is really thick and she gets a little safety pin and fastens it on. She gives me a carton of milk and a pink wafer. I just bite a little bit off the end cos I want it to last till I get back to class and I can show Debbie. She pats me on the head.

"Come on then. I'll take you home to your Mum."

"I want to stay with you, Miss. Mister Shelby will get us if we go out."

"Now listen carefully, Rebecca. Mister Shelby is not going to get you. Not when I'm with you. I'm going to report this, I swear. He won't be bothering you or any other kids ever again. When I tell them, the police might come round to your house to look at your hand."

"Please don't tell them, Miss."

"It's OK. I know some kids are scared of the police. Just tell them the truth and you'll have nothing to worry about."

"The truth, Miss?"

"Yes, tell them what Mister Shelby did and everything will be fine. You'll see."

CHAPTER
TWENTY

Miss Landers puts her arm around me and keeps it there when we walk down the corridors. The school is dead quiet. All I can hear are our footsteps. Miss Landers' footsteps sound lovely cos she's got high heels on and they go click-click. She keeps looking behind her as we walk. I know she's looking for Shelby. Miss Landers is only little and I'm afraid that Shelby will hit her with his cane and get me.

When we get outside, we walk really fast across the playground. Nobody is playing out. I don't know what time it is, but playtime must be finished cos I can see Mister Smith sweeping up paper. Mister Smith is the caretaker and he does the cleaning up, and sometimes he has to put sawdust down when we get sick. He waves at Miss Landers, but she doesn't wave back. He just carries on sweeping. When we get outside the school gates Miss Landers gives me a big smile.

She keeps her arm around me all through Piggy Monk Square. We go past the Bommy. I'd forgotten about Sniffer. I wonder if they've found him yet. I hope his friends have come and took him home. I won't think about him any more. Every time I think about him I'll hum a little song. I start humming. Miss Landers stops walking and looks at me.

"Are you OK, Rebecca?"

"Yes Miss."

She carries on walking and soon we're in our street. I hum all the way to our house. She looks up and down the street, then knocks on the door. Mam comes to the door straight away and she sees me bandages.

"Oh my God! What's happened?"

"Can I come in, please?"

"Yes. What happened? Did she fall over?"

We go inside and sit down.

"Don't worry, she's fine, but I need to talk to you in private."

They both look at me and make their eyes go little. I know what that means.

"OK. Rebecca, will you go to your room for a minute?"

I was right. I go upstairs and sit on the bed. I try to listen but they're whispering. After a while I hear the front door opening and closing and me Mam starts calling me.

When I go down she's got her chin in her hand.

"I'm sorry Mam, I didn't mean to get into trouble. I couldn't help it."

"It's all right Rebecca, Miss Landers told me all about it. It wasn't your fault. I shouldn't have slept in. That man should be locked up! Is your hand hurting you?"

"A bit."

"Well, Miss Landers says she cleaned it and bandaged it properly, so I won't take the bandages off yet. I'll have a look later, OK?"

There's a loud knock on the door. It must be the coppers. Miss Landers must have told them already and now they've come to see me hand. I hope they're nice ones like Miss Landers said. I hope they're not the kicking-coppers. I have to get me hand ready to show them, so I take the pin out and start to unwind the bandage. Me Mam runs to answer the door, but it's not coppers, it's that Auntie Mo, the witch. She's got loads and loads of perfume on and it stinks. I can smell it even though she's still standing by the door and hasn't come right the way in.

"Mo, you can come in if you want, but I'm warning you, I'm not in the mood for any more fighting."

Mo steps inside, takes one look at me hand and her big mouth opens.

"What in the name of God happened to her, Karen?"

Me bandage is all undone and me hand's got cuts on it. There's nasty dark blood on the cuts. It looks horrible, worse than a soldier and I didn't even get shot. Mam runs over to me, kneels down and stares at it.

"Jesus! Miss Landers said it was cut but I didn't think. I didn't. I'll kill him! I swear to God I'll kill him with my own bare hands!"

"It's all right, Mam. It doesn't hurt too much. Just a little bit."

"Oh you poor thing. I can't believe it."

"What happened, Karen? Who did it? Was it Brian?"

"No it wasn't Brian for God's sake! It was that Shelby, the headmaster."

Mo folds her arms and stares at me.

"Well about time too. Someone needed to sort her out. She's running wild that one."

"Mo, will you shut up?"

But Mo doesn't shut up. She never shuts up. She comes over to me and looks down at me hand. Then she turns her head to one side and shakes it.

"What did you do then, Rebecca? What did you do to deserve this?"

"She was late, that's all. Miss Landers from the school came up and told me. She didn't do anything wrong."

Mo sucks in her lips and frowns so much her eyebrows nearly join up.

"You couldn't have got that just for being late, Rebecca. You must have done something else. Come on. Tell the truth for a change. What did you do?"

"Nothing."

"Mo, I'm telling you she didn't do anything except be late. Miss Landers told me."

"Oh, and who is this Miss Landers then?"

"The school secretary. She brought our Rebecca home and she said she's going to report Shelby to the police."

"What? The police? I've never heard anything so soft in my life. As if they're going to come round here bothering themselves with bad little girls who get the cane like they deserve! We got much worse than that and it didn't do us any harm!"

"So you think it did us good?"

"Spare the rod and . . ."

"You've had it in for her ever since she was born. I don't remember you saying one nice thing to her. Not even when she was a tiny little baby in a blanket."

"Because she's bad, that's why, and you should know it. Some people are born bad and she's one of them."

"For Christ sake, Mo! There's no such thing as being born bad. How the hell can a tiny baby be bad?"

"God makes some people evil, even babies. Born evil, grow up evil and die evil. They taught us that in school."

"Jesus, Mo! You didn't take any notice of all that crap, did you? Look. Look at this."

Mam goes over to the sideboard and picks up a picture. It's me in a pram when I was very small. I'm sitting up and smiling. I've got no teeth, so I'm not pretty but I've got a lovely little bonnet on with a frill all the way round it.

"Look at this picture and tell me what's evil about it."

Mo snatches it from me Mam's hand. "Look at her eyes, Karen, look at them. They're dead sly, see, they're evil, can't you see it?"

Mam snatches the picture back and hugs it before she puts it back on the sideboard.

"You have to stop this, Mo! You have to stop it now. If you carry on like this you're going to end up in the funny farm."

190

"I won't. I'm the oldest. I know what's right and she's not right! She's not right at all! She's evil, wicked, bad — pure bad!"

Mam looks really sad for a minute but then she suddenly turns round to Auntie Mo and slaps her, right in the face. She slaps her so hard it makes Mo's face bounce.

"I told you you'd push me too far one day!"

Mo puts her hand on her face and her eyes get full of tears.

"You hit me Karen! You hit me!"

"I know I did."

"Say you're sorry!" says Mo, still holding her face.

"We're not kids, Mo."

"I said, say you're sorry!"

"I'm not sorry. I'm not a bit sorry."

"You're not supposed to hit me. I'm only little. Mam never hit me and she said you could never hit me. I've had operations!"

"I know you did Mo but that was years ago, and you've been getting away with murder ever since. Mam's dead and if you ask me she was far too soft with you . . ."

Mo tries to hit me Mam back but she misses and then she starts crying, really crying. Then she points at me.

"If it wasn't for her, our mother'd still be here. The minute she heard you got pregnant she died. Everyone in church saw you with your big belly. You made a show of her!"

Mam shakes her head and looks at Mo. "She had cancer, she'd had it for years."

"No she didn't. I would have known. She would have told me."

"She did, Mo. She did have cancer but she didn't tell you. She was trying to protect you. She was always trying to protect you."

"She never had cancer! She never!"

"It's the truth Mo. Now go home. I can't stick up for you any more. You have to keep away."

Mo opens the door but she doesn't go out.

"You promised me Mam you'd look after me. You promised on her deathbed!"

"You're big enough to look after yourself now, Mo."

Mo walks out the door and doesn't even bother closing it. Mam shuts it and puts the bolt on.

The door starts banging. Mam goes to the window and peeps out.

"It's Mo back again. We'll ignore her and she'll go away in a minute, she'll just have to learn somehow," says me Mam and she starts biting her lip and rubbing her knees. The door bangs again. Mo's really hammering on it. Mam gets up and starts bandaging me hand up again. She can't do it like Miss Landers, some bits are crooked and it doesn't look as neat. It doesn't matter though cos I'll have to take it off again to show the coppers anyway. The door keeps banging. If Mo doesn't stop soon, Nosy Noreen'll come out of her house and there'll be loads of argy-bargy. Nosy Noreen doesn't like noise.

192

"Whatever you do Rebecca, don't you take any notice of Mo. She didn't mean what she said."

"Why did she say I killed me Nan?"

"Cos she just says the first thing that comes into her head."

"Why don't any nice things come into her head?"

"I don't know. Maybe she just finds nasty things easier to say. Anyway, I'm not letting her come back, I've let her get away with far too much for far too long, so you just forget all about her."

The door stops banging. Mo must have got fed up and gone home. Mam goes to make some soup and when she comes back we both sit on the couch and watch telly. There's a film on. A Western, with lots of cowboys riding horses. One day I'm going to ride a horse just like Emma from my book. I'm going to call him Sparkle. I'm going to get a lovely stable in Sefton Park, right up near the glass house, so Sparkle will be nice and warm and he can look through the glass to see all the people walking round and look at all the lovely big gigantic plants. Me and Sparkle are going to go everywhere in the whole wide world, even New Brighton. I won't have to get the ferry cos horses can swim. The horses in this film go all the way across a big river full of rocks and waves and they have to carry loads of bundles of stuff as well. If I had a horse nobody could reach me. I'd be so high up, nobody would have arms long enough to get me, not Sniffer, not Stabber and not even Shelby.

When the film's finished, me Mam stands up and looks at her watch.

"I forgot the time, there's nothing in the house for our tea. Come on quick, if we go fast we'll make it to the baker's."

It takes ages to walk there cos it's right the way up the top of the main road, behind a gigantic block of flats. We don't mind, we always go to this one cos it's got the softest and the nicest cakes. We get the lovely cakey-pastry smell even before we get round the corner. You can't see anything through the window cos it's all covered in cardboard, but when you get inside there's huge cake mountains all over the shop. None of them are perfect. Sometimes the cherry might be missing off a cherry bun or maybe the gingerbread men are missing a leg or an arm, but we don't mind cos they're scrummy. Mam buys two pasties, some crusty cobs and two squashed lemon cakes with lovely little sugar lemons on top. The only thing that's wrong with them is that the leaves are missing off the lemons, and I don't care cos I don't like the leaves anyway.

When we get back to our street, I can see me Dad standing by our door. He's waiting for us. He should have went in with his key like he always did. I wish he would, but he just stands there waiting. Like as if it's not his house. When we get up to him he picks me up, gives me a hug and a swing around. Then he sees me hand.

"What happened to her?"

"Come in and I'll tell you."

I think Mam really wants him to stay cos she puts the pasty she got for herself on a plate and gives it to him, even though she's got none for herself now.

"I'll make some tea. Do you want some?"

"Yes please."

Dad's being nice too. He twiddles me cheek and smiles at me. "Well, what have you been up to? Did you cut your hand?"

Mam comes in with the tea and puts the pot on the table. "That headmaster, Shelby, he gave her the cane. You should see her hand Brian, it's all cut."

"What? Give us a look, Rebecca, come here."

"Wait till she's got her tea, will you? I want her to eat something."

Then they look at each other and put their little eyes on, like they know something I don't know, the way they used to do.

We put brown sauce on our pasties and eat them. Mam just eats a crusty cob.

"I'm not eating your tea am I, Karen?" asks me Dad.

"I didn't fancy it," says me Mam.

That's not true. I know she fancied the pasty cos she told me she did in the baker's. I won't tell though. I don't want me Mam and Dad falling out no more. I like us all sitting here having our tea, even if me Mam hasn't got a pasty. I cut mine in half and try to put it on her plate, but she just shakes her head. Me Dad eats his in two seconds, so Mam gets up and gets the lemon cakes and cuts them into little pieces so we can all have a bit, and as soon as we've finished she stands up.

"Go and watch the telly for a bit love."

I know they want me to go away so they can talk secrets. I don't mind cos when we were all together they used to talk secrets as well.

Boring old news is on. I turn over and there it is again. There's nothing else on so I have to watch it. The newsman's talking about some war that's going on. It's very far away from here, so we don't have to worry about bombs and soldiers running everywhere. Mam says nothing like that could happen in Liverpool. When all the war things are finished the newsman comes back on, and all of a sudden he goes away and instead there's a picture of Sniffer. A great big picture. He's smiling in the picture and he looks different, he looks nice and friendly.

The newsman comes back again and says they've found the missing policeman and that his body was left in a derelict house. Me Dad comes in and me Mam follows him. They both start looking at the telly.

"They've found him then, maybe things will get back to normal now. They've been all over the place since he went missing," says me Dad.

"I know, they called here as well, dead narky they were too," says me Mam.

"Well I suppose they were frantic."

"Yeah, but there was no need for the way they spoke to me."

"Why, what did they say?"

"Oh I'll tell you later," says me Mam, looking at me.

"Oh right, yeah," says me Dad and then he sits down and picks up me hand and starts to take the bandage off. I look at the telly again. The newsman says a man is helping police with their enquiries.

"What does helping with enquiries mean, Dad?"

196

"That means someone's in loads of trouble. I wouldn't like to be him."

"Did you hear what happened to Harold from down the street?" says me Mam.

Dad keeps unwinding the bandage. "I heard about it, there's no need for it. Bloody animals! Poor Harold's just a bit gone in the head, that's all. He didn't do anything to deserve a kicking like that."

The last bit of bandage comes off. Me hand looks even worse now. The dark blood has gone hard and there's a bit of skin peeling off to one side.

"Jesus Christ! This is really cut! What kind of a nutter would do that to a little girl?"

"That's what I said," says me Mam.

"So this Miss Landers, she said she was going to the police then?"

"Yeah, she was great, she said she was going straight round there after she left our house. She reckoned they'd probably come round to see our Rebecca's hand."

"And there's been no sign of them?"

"Not so far. We went up to the baker's though, maybe we missed them."

"Ask Nosy Noreen if they've been, she's bound to know."

"I don't want her knowing our business, Brian."

"I'd say she knows what we had for tea by now. Go on. Go and ask her, tell her Rebecca had a little accident, that's all."

"Oh, OK then."

Mam goes out and Dad sits me on his knee.

"We'll get this sorted for you. No one's hitting my girl like that and getting away with it."

"Miss Landers said all I had to do was tell the truth to the coppers and everything would be all right."

"Well Miss Landers sounds like she's got sense."

"Miss Landers is lovely Dad."

"I know pet, she looked after you so she must be."

Mam comes back in. "No, she said there was loads of coppers up and down the street all afternoon, seventeen, she said, but none of them knocked on our door."

"They must be coming tonight then. I want to be here when they come. I want to talk to them as well. Is it OK if I stay for a bit?"

"OK, to be honest I didn't fancy talking to them on my own. Not after the last time anyway." Then she says to me, "Rebecca, why don't you go and do some cutting-out on the table?"

"I don't want to play cutting-out, I want to sit here with you and me Dad."

"Tell you what love, if you're good and do some cutting-out I'll go the shop and get us some pop," says me Dad.

"And crisps?"

"Yeah, go on then."

I run into the kitchen and me Mam gets an old newspaper and me little scissors. Mam's got a big huge scissors but I'm not allowed to play with them. She keeps them in a drawer in the kitchen cupboard. Sometimes when she's not there I take them out and look at them, they're lovely and shiny and they're real

198

gold. I never use them for me cutting-out cos Mam says they're so sharp they'd cut the hand off me. I hear the front door closing and I know me Dad's gone the shop, just like he promised.

I draw a picture of me Mam on the newspaper, then I cut it out so I've got a paper doll of me Mam. Then I make one of me Dad and then I make one of me. I stand them all up, but they're too soft and they just fall down. In school we make them out of cardboard, but we haven't got any at home so I have to get a bowl and lean them up against it to make them stand up. I put me Dad on one side, me Mam on the other and me in the middle. I'm going to make a house next. I draw a big square on the paper, like Miss Chambers showed me, and then two windows and a door. It hasn't got a roof, but I'm not very good at drawing roofs so I just make another square on top. I squidge up the paper and cut the windows out so they open, and then I do the same with the door. I take the paper dolls down and put the house against the bowl. Then I open the door and the windows and put the dolls behind them so it looks like we're all peeping out. Me Mam's peeping out the bottom window, I'm peeping out the top one and me Dad's peeping out the door. These are the best ones I've ever made and I'm dead pleased. They don't fall down either.

I hear the front door open and shut and me Dad comes in. Him and me Mam come out to the kitchen and they pour out the pop, a glass each for all of us. Me Dad hands me a packet of cheese and onion crisps. He has two packets of smoky bacon for him and me Mam.

"Watcha doing there then, Rebecca?" asks me Dad.

"I made us, Dad, and I made a house and put us in it," I say and show him.

Mam comes over to look. It doesn't make them smile though. They both look sad. Mam doesn't say anything, doesn't even say it's good. She just goes into the living room.

Dad says, "Very good love," then squeezes me shoulder and follows me Mam.

They're talking really quietly. I bet they're talking about me cut-outs. They didn't think they were lovely, not one bit. I have to make better ones. This time I'll be really careful. I didn't use the ruler to draw the house last time and it got a bit crooked, so I run upstairs to get me ruler. I draw another house. This one's much better. The ruler makes it come out all nice and straight. I need to be really careful cutting it out. Me little scissors don't really cut all that straight. Me Mam sometimes makes things, like curtains, and when she does she uses the big scissors and she always cuts out straight. I think I'll get the big scissors from the drawer. If I'm really careful they won't know and when they see how straight the house is they'll be really pleased with me. I tiptoe to the cupboard and get the scissors and tiptoe back to the table.

"What are you doing with those scissors?" It's me Mam. "Here, give them to me. Do you want cuts on your other hand as well? You know quite well you're not supposed to touch those scissors. They'd cut the hand off you."

200

She takes the scissors away from me and puts them back in the drawer.

"Never, ever go near that drawer again. Do you hear me Rebecca?"

"Yes Mam. I'm sorry. I just wanted the house to be straight that's all."

"Give us a look then," she says and picks up the paper. Then she goes back to the drawer and gets her scissors and cuts the house out for me.

"There you are. That's nice and straight. You get finished with your cutting-out cos it's time for bed soon."

"But I'm supposed to wait for the coppers and show them me hand."

"There's no sign of them and we can't keep you up all night, you've got school tomorrow."

"I don't want to go to school. Shelby will get me and cut me other hand."

"No he won't. Now go on, finish off your cutting-out."

There's a knock on the door. Mam runs out and I follow her. Me Dad opens the door. It's Miss Landers. She looks upset.

"Oh, what's up with you love? Come in, come in," says me Dad.

Miss Landers comes in. She looks at me and starts to cry.

"What's the matter?" asks me Dad.

"Did you go to the police?" asks me Mam.

Miss Landers just nods.

"And are they going to come round to see her hand?"

Miss Landers shakes her head and starts crying even more.

"Rebecca, go to bed," says me Dad.

"But, Dad."

"Do as you're told, off you go."

"Go on, Rebecca, do like your Dad says."

"But Mam, I haven't done me teeth and I haven't had a wash."

"Go on into the kitchen and wash your face, then do your teeth. Then go straight to bed and I'll be up in a minute," says me Mam.

I brush me teeth and wash me face. I have to do it in cold water cos me Mam didn't leave any hot water in the kettle for me. I hate getting washed in cold water. It doesn't really get your face proper clean. I didn't finish making me paper dolls either. I wanted to make lovely cut-outs of us looking all happy in the house. Then Mam and Dad would see that it's better when we all live here, all together.

CHAPTER
TWENTY-ONE

When I wake up me Dad is sitting on the bed. He's stroking me head.

"Come on, up you get love, I'm taking you to school today."

"Did the coppers come?"

"No love, they didn't."

"Why not?"

"Cos they don't care about people like us, that's why."

"Why? Why don't they care about us?"

"Never you mind. Come on, up you get. Your Mam's made egg on toast for us all. It'll be going cold."

We only have egg on toast for breakfast when me Mam's in a really good mood. I put on me clothes as fast as I can and run down the stairs. They're both sitting at the table and they're both smiling. Me Dad pulls a lump off his toast and dips it into his egg. I do the same, then me Mam does too. We all laugh cos the egg's runny and it falls off the toast and back on the plate. We all rip another bit of bread off and dip it on the plate at exactly the same time, then we all laugh again. I love this game. We always do this when we have egg on toast. We have to see who's finished first and then we have to check the plate to make sure there's no egg left on. Me Dad always wins. It's hard to win at this game cos you have to make sure you still have a bit of toast to wipe up the last bit of egg on the plate. If you haven't that means you have a dirty plate. You're not allowed to use your fingers cos that's cheating. Me Dad is really careful when he rips his toast, he always counts the pieces to make sure there's enough left. He comes first, me Mam comes second and I come last. I don't care. I always come last at this game. That's the way it is.

When we've finished, me Mam clears the table and me Dad helps her. That's funny. He never does that. Mam always does it and sometimes I help.

"How come me Dad's taking me to school?"

"He's got to talk to them and see what's going on, that's why."

"What about Miss Landers? Will she be there?"

"No love, she's not working there any more."

"Why not?"

"She has to get a new job, that's why."

"Why? Why can't she work at our school the way she always did?"

"She can't, Rebecca."

"When she gets her new job can I go to that school?"

"Oh God, Rebecca, I don't know. We'll have to wait and see. Now quick, get ready. Your Dad's waiting for you."

Me Dad stands up and I can see he's not got any shoes on. He couldn't have come down the road to our house this morning in just his socks. He must have stayed here last night.

"Dad. Dad. Did you sleep here last night?"

"I did, love."

"Are you back home Dad? Are you back home for good?"

But he doesn't answer. Mam turns away and he just starts putting his shoes on.

"Are you back home Dad?"

"Wait and see, love. Wait and see."

Dad holds me hand all the way to school. I swing me hand to see if he'll swing too, but he doesn't. We just walk quietly along. We go past the Bommy. There's a new thing all around it. I don't know what it is. It's a bit like a tent only bigger. We can't see in. There's two coppers standing there watching us go past. I'm not scared though, cos me Dad's with me. He gives them a dirty look and they give him one back.

When we get close to our school gate, Dad stops. There's loads of kids rushing into school, but we just stand there and watch them for a minute.

"Right then, come on Rebecca. We're going in," says Dad.

I go to walk in but he doesn't move, just keeps standing still like a big statue.

"I thought you said we were going in then, Dad?"

"Yeah in a sec," he says and he bends down to tie his shoelaces even though they're already tied.

"OK, ready?" he says, shaking his shoulders.

We walk in and all the kids behind us get in a line and follow. They don't push and shove cos me Dad's there. It's great cos it's kinda like being the leader of a great big band or a great big army.

When we get inside they all go the other way. We're going to Shelby's office. On the way we meet Miss Chambers and she stops when she sees me Dad.

"Oh hello, you must be Rebecca's dad?"

"Yeah."

"I'm Miss Chambers, Rebecca's teacher. Can I help you?"

"No, we're going to see Mister Shelby."

"I'm afraid Mister Shelby doesn't like to be interrupted in the mornings."

"I bet he doesn't," says me Dad and keeps going.

When we get to Shelby's office Dad goes straight in. He doesn't knock on the door or anything. Mister Shelby is sitting at his desk and he's reading a magazine. He puts it in his drawer when he sees us.

"Are you Shelby?"

"I am Mister Shelby and I would prefer it if in future you did me the courtesy of knocking."

"Oh would you now? Well I'd prefer it if you did me the courtesy of keeping your filthy hands off my kid!"

Shelby picks up the phone off his desk. Dad grabs it and holds it in his arms.

"Give me back that phone," says Shelby.

"No! Not till you've listened to what I've got to say," says me Dad.

"You can jolly well leave my office. You have not made an appointment. I am a very busy man."

"Yeah, busy beating up little kids."

"I do not beat up children. I discipline them. Discipline is an essential part of any school if order is to be maintained. Especially, may I add, in an inner-city area. It is as important for your daughter's education as reading and writing. She will need discipline and self-control for any job, even the most menial."

"Shut up! I want to know have the police been to see you?"

"Why on earth would the police come to see me?"

"Because of what you did to my Rebecca."

"No. The police do not waste their time entering schools and investigating matters which, after all, are purely matters of education."

Shelby picks up a big red book from his desk and starts moving his finger down the page and looking at me.

"Looking at her reports, I suggest you concentrate on helping Rebecca with her arithmetic. She is in danger of falling behind. Some parental guidance might be of some use."

"My Rebecca's always done all right in school so far."

"All right is a relative term. All right will not get her to university. All right will not get her into any respectable profession." Shelby picks up a pen and taps the red book with it.

"What are you on about? She's not ten yet and you're trying to say she won't get into university. How would you know?"

"Experience tells me."

"Oh, and I suppose belting her with the cane will get her into university. You hit her too hard. Her hand was bleeding you know."

"Nonsense."

"It's not nonsense. Miss Landers brought her home and told my wife. Miss Landers says she saw you."

"Ah, Miss Landers. Well I'm sorry that Miss Landers took it upon herself to interfere and I'm certain it won't happen again."

"She told us you gave her the sack. Tried to make out she stole some dinner money didn't you?"

"The excuses people make. Very sad. The way these people always try to blame others for their own actions. I personally left her in charge of the dinner money and on my return she was unable to account for it."

"You just got rid of her because she went to the police."

"Of course she made ridiculous claims about me in order to distract attention from her crime. That's what liars and thieves do."

"Miss Landers is lovely, Dad. Don't take any notice of him," I say, even though I'm supposed to keep quiet. I don't want me Dad to believe those nasty things.

"She managed to fool a lot of people and of course children are the easiest to fool, especially those who are less fortunate."

"Less fortunate! What the hell do you mean by that?"

"Let us just say, less academically gifted."

"I don't know what you're on about. Talk plain English will you?"

Mister Shelby smiles and puts his two hands together so his fingers hold on to each other.

"I'm sorry. Let me explain. Now, the truth is, your daughter was late for school, received a light tap or two with the cane, which I might add is perfectly within the bounds of my duty and, of course, the law. Apparently when Miss Landers took it upon herself to bring Rebecca home, the child fell and then, I'm afraid, Miss Landers concocted this elaborate yarn in an attempt to place blemish on my character. Luckily the police totally understood once I explained the situation."

Dad starts fiddling with his collar.

"What situation?"

"Miss Landers comes from a family who are, let's say, known to the police."

"That's not her fault is it? She was dead nice to our Rebecca."

Shelby ignores what me Dad says and just keeps going on and on. It's like me Dad's not even there.

"We were aware of this prior to her employment, but in the interests of fairness we gave her the opportunity to earn an honest living. The police are aware that my own reputation is impeccable both as a headmaster and as a respectable member of the community."

"Dad, he's always hitting us, and he hits Robbie all the time. For nothing!"

Shelby writes something down in his book and stands up.

Me Dad's still holding onto Shelby's phone, he puts it under his arm and grabs me hand. He undoes the bandage and holds me hand out towards Shelby.

"Look at her, look at her hand. That's what you did. There's no way a fall would make cuts like that."

But Shelby hardly looks, just shakes his head.

"Tut. Tut. Tut. That is jolly unpleasant. I am afraid you must take up this matter with Miss Landers."

Dad keeps holding me hand out.

"No, look at her hand, there's no way she got that from falling. No way!"

"I'm afraid she must have."

"You're a liar! First of all you said the police hadn't been round here, then you said you'd 'explained the situation' to them."

"Ah yes, well as I said, they did not attend here. I had no choice but to go to the police station myself. It was my duty to report a theft. Just as it would be my duty to report any threatening behaviour that occurs in my office."

"Oh here we go! And what do you mean by that?"

"Well here you are, without invitation, removing my telephone and using abusive and threatening language."

"Bollocks!"

"Exactly."

"I'm going to take her out of this school. I've had enough of this. No one's going to hit my Rebecca like that."

"Dad! Dad!" I say, jumping up and down.

"What?"

"Can I go to Miss Landers' new school?"

"That will be impossible. Miss Landers will never be employed in an educational institution again."

"I'll keep her home," says me Dad.

"Then you would certainly be breaking the law."

"Jesus Christ!"

"I can assure you that if Rebecca continues with her education in this school, she will receive only the best of care and attention."

"You're not touching her! Do you hear me?"

"If it would put your mind at rest, I can leave all matters of discipline to her class teacher and . . . I will say no more about your own conduct in entering my office without permission, not to mention the attempted theft of school property."

"What theft? What school property?"

Shelby coughs and looks at the phone me Dad's still got under his arm. Dad takes the phone and puts it down on the table.

"Thank you, now if that will be all . . ."

"Right well, er, you just remember, don't touch her, not ever," says me Dad and takes me by the hand and brings me to the door.

When we get outside Shelby's office Dad puts his hand in his hair and runs it backwards and forwards. "Come on love," he says. "I'm taking you to class."

"But Dad! Mister Shelby might get me when you're gone."

"Oh he won't, don't you worry. He won't go near you."

But he doesn't sound definitely sure.

"No Dad, don't leave me here, he might get me."

"Nobody's going to get you. Just you be good."

"But I was good. I didn't mean to be late."

"I know love, just be as good as you can," says me Dad and takes me to our class. He knocks on the door and Miss Chambers comes over.

"You take care of her, will you? Don't let that Shelby near her. I'm warning you, don't let him touch her again," he says in a quiet voice.

"Of course. Come on, Rebecca, go and sit down," says Miss Chambers and she starts gulping and swallowing, like she's got something stuck in her throat. I go and sit down beside Debbie. Miss Chambers goes to the board and starts pointing to some sums. I look at the door. Me Dad's still there. He's standing really still, looking at me. I think he's going to come back and get me, but he doesn't. He just walks away and leaves me.

CHAPTER
TWENTY-TWO

It's sums again. Miss Chambers puts them on the board and as usual we have to copy them down and then we have to find the answers. She comes over and lifts up me book.

"All wrong, Rebecca. All wrong! Weren't you listening?"

"I was Miss. I was trying, Miss."

"OK, Rebecca, now look carefully."

Miss Chambers works out one sum and then tells me to do the other, the same as she did, but I can't remember what she said. I get it wrong and she puts a big X on me book and it spoils the page.

"You weren't paying attention, Rebecca. Go and sit on the naughty table at once."

So I have to go and sit on the naughty table. Robbie Renshaw's there already. He gives me a little grin cos he's pleased he doesn't have to sit on his own. We're not there long when Miss Chambers rings her little bell.

"Now, girls and boys, we're going to the hall," she says, smiling at everyone except me. When we get into the hall, Miss Chambers kneels down and starts fiddling with a record player in the corner. First of all it crackles and makes scratchy noises, but then these big trumpets start playing.

"Now! I want you to march like little soldiers to the end of the hall, and when I say 'Turn' I want you to march back. Swing your arms backwards and forwards, like this," she shouts and does her arms like a soldier.

We all set off marching like soldiers to the end of the hall. When we get there we forget to wait for her to say "Turn" and we all turn around and start marching back again.

"No! No! Stop! I haven't said 'Turn' yet. Come back and start again," she shouts.

We all run back to the start and do it again, but even though she just reminded us, we forget to wait for her to say "Turn" again. We're all in a big rush to see who can get there first. She gets fed up and goes over to the record player and changes the record. The new record is much nicer. The song is kind of soft and there's a woman singing in a really high voice. This time we have to pretend to be little clouds floating in the sky, and we have to jump in the air whenever Miss Chambers shouts "Rainbow".

We don't do that right either cos Gerry Smith starts pretending to be a tank and goes round bumping into everyone. We all copy him and then Miss Chambers goes mad and starts shouting, "No! No! No! Make a line! Make a line!"

We all get in a big line. I'm the very last in the line except for one. Robbie Renshaw is still running around the hall. He's still pretending to be a cloud and he's running and jumping all over the place. He's smiling and smiling. I've never seen him do a big smile before.

"Robbie Renshaw! You again! Come here at once and line up!"

Robbie comes running over and just before he gets to the end of the line he does a gigantic big jump in the air and shouts "Rainbow!"

"Oh come along, back to class, the lot of you. And as for you, Robbie, you'll be on the naughty table tomorrow as well," says Miss Chambers, but I don't think Robbie cares cos he's still smiling.

She reads us a story about these kids who have adventures. They go off to a big cave and they find loads of fossils. Fossils are worms and snails and strange creatures from the olden days that got stuck in the middle of stones. The kids in the story find lots and lots of them and they're really pleased, like as if they found treasure or something. Every time they find a fossil they say, "Gosh, golly and super." We all laugh when they say that and Miss Chambers slams the book on the table.

"I don't know what it is that's supposed to be so funny! Be quiet all of you, before I fetch Mister Sh . . . before I make you all write out fifty lines." She picks up the book and starts reading again, so we all go quiet and cover our mouths with our hands whenever she says, "Gosh, golly and super."

Suddenly she stops reading and says, "Don't any of you like this story? Any of you? Any of you at all?"

"Miss, I do, I love stories," shouts Robbie and we all shout and nod as well. She smiles then and reads the rest. In the end everything's really happy cos the girls and boys go back to their house and have hot chocolate and sticky buns.

"Wasn't that a nice story, girls and boys?"

"Yes, Miss," we all shout out, cos it was really, well better than sums. I'd rather have stories than sums any day. I love stories. I think when I get big I'm going to make up loads of stories, nice stories with lots of horses and treasure, and write them in books with lovely pictures, and I'll live in a lovely house with me Mam and Dad and Sparkle and a slide and a swing and we'll have loads of hot chocolate and sticky buns.

After dinner we learn all about oak leaves and oak trees and draw pictures of them in our drawing books. I don't really like drawing oak trees and oak leaves cos you can only use green and brown. So I draw a big load of flowers growing out of them, all different colours, red and purple and blue and yellow. Miss Chambers doesn't give me a star though cos she says flowers don't grow on oak trees.

I can't wait for the bell to go cos I want to go home and see if me Dad's there. Debbie has to go straight home too cos her Mam's taking her into town to get new curtains out of all the money her Dad won. She's going fast, but when we get round the corner away from the other kids I stop her.

"It said on the telly they found him."

"I know. Me Dad said it served the pig right and he feels sorry for the fella that's getting done for it, cos if you touch a pig you've had it!"

"Then we've had it as well!"

"No! It wasn't us! It was that old tramp. We didn't do nothing!"

"But he was already dead when the tramp came along."

"We might have been wrong. We didn't have one of them things the doctors have, you know, the long metal things for listening to hearts. That Sniffer was dead sneaky, he was probably pretending to be dead so he could catch us and then the old tramp came and really murdered him."

"Do you think so?"

"Yeah, me Dad said he heard that they found Sniffer's wallet in the old tramp's pocket and he must have robbed him as well."

"What do you . . . ?"

"Shush," whispers Debbie. We're passing right by the Bommy now and the two coppers are looking at us. Another copper comes out the door of the tent and says something to one of them. They all go back inside.

"Come on, leg it!" says Debbie.

And we run all the way till we get to our street. Just before she goes in, Debbie grabs me by the arm.

"You'd never grass us up, would you?"

"Never."

"Me Dad says there's only one thing worse than a grass and that's a pig."

"Did you tell your Dad, Debbie?"

"No, I promised I wouldn't tell, didn't I? Did you tell yours?"

"No, I never. I swear. Let's link fingers again, to make double-treble sure."

"OK."

She puts her little finger out and so do I. When we link them together, we give them an extra big shake. That way, no matter what happens, we'll never ever tell.

"Right then, I have to run in cos me Mam'll go mad if I make her late for the shops. See ya tomorrow then, Sparra," says Debbie, running into her house.

"Tara, Debbie."

I feel really hungry, but when I get near our house I smell liver and onions frying and I don't feel so hungry any more. Mam's in the kitchen and she's turning the pieces of liver over in the pan so they don't burn.

"Well? How did you get on in school?"

"OK, we did sums and marching and oak trees and stories."

"Did that Mister Shelby come near you then?"

"No."

"Your Dad told me he sorted him out. Is your hand sore?"

"No, just a little bit stingy sometimes."

"Good, come here then and give us a kiss."

She gives me kisses all over me face and then she remembers the liver and starts turning it all over again.

"Why do we have to have liver for dinner?"

"Cos it's your Dad's favourite."

"Me Dad's coming for dinner?"

"Yes he is."

"Have you and me Dad made friends again?"

"Yes we have."

"Is he staying with us now?"

Mam nods her head up and down.

"Is he staying with us for ever and ever?"

"I hope so love, but I don't know how long for ever is. Now you go and get your uniform off. He'll be here soon."

I run upstairs and pull me uniform off and throw it on the floor so I can get down the stairs quicker to wait for me Dad.

"You go and sweep the living room so it will be nice for your Dad."

"Yes Mam."

I go to the cupboard under the stairs and get the sweeper out. I sweep everywhere in the whole room, even under the couch cos I want it to be perfect. Then I get the duster and dust everywhere I can reach, even the wallpaper.

I see me Dad coming past the window and I jump up to meet him at the door. I hear him opening the door. He's got his key! He must be staying.

"Hello, sunshine," he says.

"Hiya Dad. Are you staying with us now, Dad? Have you and me Mam made friends again? Are you staying for ever and ever and ever and ever?"

CHAPTER
TWENTY-THREE

I've got both me arms tight around me Dad's neck. He can't go away even if he wanted to.

"Yes love, I'm staying for ever and ever and ever," he says with a lovely smile, and he gives me a big hug and a big wet kiss with sucky noises as well.

"How did you get on in school? That Shelby didn't come near you did he?"

"No Dad."

"Were you good?"

"I was dead, dead good Dad."

"Well then, if you can guess which hand the pressie's in I'll give it to you."

Then he puts both his hands behind his back, shuffles them around, then squidges them into fists and holds them out towards me. I tap one hand and he opens it. It's empty! So I tap the other one. It's empty too.

"You're cheating! It's not fair!"

"I'm only messing with you, love. Tell you what, watch this."

He puts both hands behind his back again and shuffles them some more. Then he holds out one hand towards me and opens it up. Inside is the tiniest little doll I've ever seen. It's perfect though and she's wearing a little hat and a coat and even little shoes, red ones, red shiny ones.

"There, that's for being a good girl."

"Thanks, Dad, she's the best doll I've ever seen."

Dad's still holding out his hand and I see his wedding ring. Oh God I forgot! I run upstairs really quick and tiptoe into me Mam and Dad's room. I pull the lino up and take out me Mam's rings, then run downstairs into the kitchen.

"Here you are Mam. Dad's back now and you can put your rings on and we won't have any bad luck any more."

"I hope not love, I've had just about as much bad luck as I can take," she says and looks at them for a minute before she puts them on. Just in time cos me Dad comes into the kitchen.

"What did you run away for? Didn't you like your new doll?"

"I forgot to hang me uniform up," I say, telling a little fib.

"God love, you've changed," he says.

Mam gives me an empty matchbox and I put the new doll inside. It's just the right size to make a bed for her. Mam says she's going to get some material and she'll make a blanket for her so she'll be nice and warm too. I'm going to call me new doll Dottie, cos she's got a dotty dress on under her little coat. Mam calls us for dinner and we all sit down at the table. When I look at me plate I can't believe it, cos there's no liver! Instead, beside the potatoes, there's a big heap of baked beans. I love baked beans and I eat them all up while they eat that stringy old smelly liver.

After our dinner, we go in the living room with our tea and me Mam brings in some biscuits. Everything's really ordinary again, just like it used to be. Me Dad puts on the telly and he starts watching the news. The newsman is talking about the wars again. There's loads of them, everywhere except here. Even in Ireland, though me Dad says the trouble's not in the whole of Ireland, just in a little bit of it, the little bit at the top. Dad says Ireland is a gigantic country, bigger than New Brighton.

Suddenly there's that big picture of Sniffer again. A man of no fixed abode has been arrested and charged with murder. They don't know the man's name yet cos he won't tell them.

"Does that mean he'll go to jail for ever and ever, Dad?"

"Dead right he will, that's if they don't kill him first."

"Who would kill him, Dad?"

"Never you mind, sunshine."

"Dad, what if it was only an accident? Would he still get sent to jail for ever?"

"That's a funny question, they didn't say it was an accident, they said it was murder."

"I know Dad, but what if he just fell and they thought it was murder?"

"Well they'd know if he just fell, then it would be an accident. But it's not though cos they're charging someone with murder."

"They might be wrong though, they might have made a mistake."

"Yeah well you'd never know with that lot."

"So if they found out it was only an accident, they wouldn't have to send him to jail then would they?"

"God, Rebecca! What's got into you with all these questions about this copper? Did you hear somebody talking about it?" says me Dad, frowning at me.

"Oh, she's just curious that's all. You know what kids are like. She doesn't know anything about it. Do you Rebecca?" says me Mam.

They're both staring and staring at me and I can feel me cheeks getting hotter and hotter. I can't answer cos this isn't a fib, it's not even a little lie, this is a great big lie and I don't want to tell it. I don't want to tell a lie that's so big I'd have to go to Hell for ever so the Devil can keep sticking a big hot fork in me all the time to make me cry. But I don't want to snitch on Debbie either. I promised and I linked fingers as well. Me Mam and Dad look at each other and then start looking at me again. They've both got their asking-things faces on.

"Rebecca? What's going on? Did you hear something?" asks me Dad.

"Leave her Brian, she doesn't know anything."

"No, look at her face, look at her, there's something wrong."

"Leave it alone Brian, for Christ sake! Can't we just have our tea in peace?" Mam's voice is getting higher, like she's going to start fighting with me Dad. I don't want them to fight. I don't want me Dad to go away again. I don't want to tell them but I don't want to tell a great big lie! The next minute, me mouth opens by itself and I'm trying to say something, but I start crying and I can't talk right.

"Jesus! What's wrong Rebecca?" says Mam.

I can't answer, so I just shake me head.

"Tell us Rebecca. Whatever it is, it'll be OK, come on, tell us. Did something happen?" asks me Dad. I shake me head again.

"Did someone say something to you?" asks me Mam.

Me voice comes back again and I can't stop it. "He fell. He fell down the ladder."

"Who fell? Who fell? Tell us Rebecca," says me Dad.

"Sniffer."

"Who's Sniffer when he's at home? A dog or something?"

"No he's not a dog, he's a pig."

"A pig?"

"What are you talking about? Pigs? Is this a story or something?"

"A great big one, he was enormous."

"Rebecca, there's no pigs round here. What are you on about?"

"The man off the telly, the one who got murdered, he fell."

"The copper?"

"Yeah, only he wasn't nice like in the picture. He was horrible and he said he'd put handcuffs on us and take us away!"

"Are you making this up?" asks me Mam.

"Tell the truth now, Rebecca," says me Dad.

224

"I'm not telling a lie. We were playing in the Bommy and he followed us and he was horrible and then he fell down the ladder and he was lying there. We didn't do it. Honest to God. He fell all by himself."

"Where Rebecca? Whereabouts?"

"In the Bommy. In Piggy Monk Square. That house that's got the tent thing over it."

"Rebecca, if you're making this up you'll be in terrible trouble. Now listen to me, you have to tell us the truth." Dad's staring into me eyes and he looks different, he looks scared.

"It is the truth. I'm not telling a big lie. It was our house, me and Debbie's. We cleaned it all up and we were going to play there, just me and Debbie and nobody else, and then he came along and he fell down the ladder into the cellar. He didn't get up so we ran away. Then when we went back he was still there and he mustn't have been able to get up the ladder."

"Why didn't you tell us?" asks Mam, chewing her lip.

"Cos we didn't want to go to jail for ever and ever."

They both go really quiet and keep looking at each other and then looking at me.

"No, she must be making it up. They've arrested somebody for it, they're saying it was murder."

"It was an old tramp. We saw him. He had loads of coats on and strings round his neck. He had dirty hair as well. He came in one day and me and Debbie had to go and hide. He went down the ladder and then we ran home so he wouldn't get us."

"Karen, they did say on the telly it was a man of no fixed abode," says me Dad.

"I know love, but she heard it as well, she could be just making it up."

"You said Debbie was with you, was she?"

"Yeah Dad, she was."

"How come she didn't tell anyone either?"

"We promised we wouldn't cos she said we'd be in loads of trouble and she said her Dad said we should never help coppers."

"That sounds like something he'd say all right," says me Mam.

"Dead right he would, he's away more than he's home," says me Dad.

"Did the policeman say anything to you Rebecca?"

"He said his leg was broke and he wanted his radio. We gave it to him. We thought he'd ring the other coppers to come and help him, but he mustn't have done cos he was still there when we went back, only this time he . . ."

"This time what Rebecca? Tell us the truth," says me Dad.

"He was really quiet and didn't even move a little bit. I think the radio was broke and that's why the others didn't come and get him."

All of a sudden me Mam stands up. She stares all around the room, like she's looking for something.

"I think she's been having bad dreams Brian."

"Have you been having bad dreams, love?"

"I dreamed all about the coppers coming and taking me away, like Harold. And another night I dreamed that me Mam and Josie were hanging up on hooks."

226

"Did you see what happened with Harold? Were you awake Rebecca?"

"I was looking out the window and he was pushing the pram and I threw me hand grenade and then the coppers came and they kicked him and kicked him and they didn't stop kicking him for ages and ages."

"Jesus! No wonder she's been having bad dreams."

"Listen Rebecca, all that stuff about the Bommy and the copper. It was all a dream. Do you understand? It wasn't real. None of that happened. That copper was murdered by some man, some tramp. It's got nothing to do with you," says me Dad.

"Yeah Rebecca, it was just a dream, no, a nightmare," says me Mam, and me Dad starts nodding his head up and down.

Me head's banging now. I didn't want anyone to find out, but now I do. I know I promised Debbie but I don't want that old man to be killed as well. It's not fair. It was an accident. Nobody should be getting killed or sent to jail for ever. I should have told them before. Now they won't believe me, but they have to believe me. I want them to make it so I don't have to think about it any more. I want them to make everything all right again. I have to tell the truth. Mam and Dad'll fix it now, now that they're back together and we're a proper family again.

"No Dad, honest to God. I swear it was real, it didn't happen in the night-time, it happened after school."

"No love, you're just mixed up, that's all, isn't she Brian?" says me Mam.

Dad doesn't answer. He keeps frowning and staring at me.

"Isn't she Brian? It was a nightmare, wasn't it Brian?"

Me Dad nods his head, but only a little bit.

"Come on Rebecca, it's time you were in bed," says me Mam and takes me by the hand into the kitchen. She pours water out of the kettle into the bowl and gets a flannel and soap and washes me face and hands.

"Now you go upstairs and get into bed and we'll come up in a minute and tuck you in."

"Am I in trouble, Mam?"

"No, no, you can't get in trouble for having a nightmare."

"But Mam . . ."

"Listen, shush about all that. Do you hear me? Shush."

I get Dottie in her little matchbox and go up. When I get to the top of the stairs I go into me room and put me nightie on, then I tiptoe back to the top of the stairs and sit down on the top step.

I hear me Mam in the kitchen. She's filling the kettle and putting it on again. Then I hear me Dad going in to her and she starts talking.

"It's because we split up, it's bad dreams that's all. It's no wonder with everything that's been going on, and seeing that poor Harold and everything," says me Mam.

"I don't know, she looked like she really believed it," says me Dad.

228

"Well, she would believe it, wouldn't she? Kids often believe nightmares are real. Remember that time she woke up and she said there was a green man under her bed? We had to search the room from top to bottom before she'd go back to sleep. Remember? Remember, Brian?"

"I do remember, but this was different. I think I'll go up and see she's OK."

"Don't let her keep going on about it, it'll only make it worse."

"I think it could get a lot worse than this," says me Dad.

I hear me Dad put his foot on the bottom step and I run back into me room and jump into bed. Dad comes in and looks around. He sees me clothes on the floor.

He picks up me uniform and puts it on the hanger. Then he lifts it up and smells it.

"Is it smelly, Dad?"

He puts his face in it and smells it again. "Nah, it smells lovely."

"Does it? What's it smell like?"

"Like little girl," he says with a sad face. I can see his eyes, there's water in them.

"I'm really, really sorry, Dad."

"I know, love." He starts to straighten the uniform and brushes a few crumbs off it, then he puts it down and puts his arm round me.

"Listen Rebecca, that story, about the policeman, you'd better not tell anybody else that story. Keep it secret. Promise me. Keep it secret for ever!"

"I promise. Honest to God. But Dad, it wasn't a dream. Really, really. It was an accident. He did fall down the ladder and then we . . ."

"Shush now pet, no more. Go to sleep and tomorrow you'll have forgotten all about it."

I put me little finger round his and shake it, three times to make sure.

Dad takes the biggest breath I've ever heard and tucks me blankets all around me, so tight that I can hardly move me arms.

"No getting up to look out the window now love. Just go straight asleep," he says. Then he goes downstairs and I know he's going to whisper to me Mam.

CHAPTER
TWENTY-FOUR

Next thing I know the light comes on and me Dad's tapping me on the shoulder. "Wake up Rebecca." I feel dozy and before I can wake up properly, he lifts me out. I sit on the side of the bed, then Mam comes in and she stands me up and starts dressing me. They don't say anything, but keep rushing around, grabbing clothes and stuffing them into a bag.

"What are you doing? Where are you taking me things? Are you sending me away to jail?"

They both stop and look at each other. Dad picks up Dottie and puts her in me hand. "Here, take your doll," he says. I feel his hand on mine, it's really warm and sticky. They both start running round the room again, opening drawers and taking things out and putting them back, it's like they're going round in circles. Then I hear the sound of a car stopping outside our house. Dad runs to the window. He pulls the curtains back a tiny bit, like the way I do when I'm making a little peephole to watch the street, then he looks out quickly and shuts the curtains again.

"Is that the coppers? Are they coming to get me?"

"No love, it's a taxi."

"For us?"

"Yeah."

"Where are we going?"

"On a trip, now come on quick. We have to go, now."

When we get down the stairs there's lots of bags in the living room. Dad opens the front door and goes out to the taxi. He says something to the taxi man. I sit on the step and watch while me Dad runs in and out of the house, bringing bags out to the taxi. The step feels really cold. I can feel it through me clothes. The step has never felt that cold before and I've never seen our street so empty before either. It doesn't look like our street. I look up and down, and even though it's dark I can see the houses are still the same, the shop's still there, the lamp-posts are in exactly the same places too, I can even see the black place in the road where the bonfire was, but still it's different. Maybe it's cos all the curtains are shut and everybody's asleep except us. It looks like all the houses have gone asleep too. There's a smell, a funny smell, a bit like stale biscuits. I can't tell where it's coming from. It seems to be everywhere, it's like it's the smell of the air but I never noticed it before.

The taxi man gets out and starts to help Dad throw all the bags inside. Mam comes and stands in the doorway behind me. I get off the step and stand up. Mam steps out and takes hold of the door as if she's going to shut it, but she doesn't. She stands looking in through the door, into the house. She makes a little noise in her throat, like a cough mixed with a swallow, and I hear her take a big breath. She pulls the door, slowly, as if she doesn't really want to shut it. Dad comes over to her and puts his arm around her.

232

"It will be OK, I promise," he says. He takes her fingers off the door, one by one, then he pulls the rest of her hand away and holds on to it as he closes the door.

Mam turns her head away real quick, like she doesn't want to look at the door any more.

"Where to?" says the taxi man.

"Pier Head, please mate," says me Dad and he holds the taxi door open for me and me Mam to climb in.

"Are we going to New Brighton? Are we going to New Brighton?"

"Yes love," says me Mam.

"What about school?"

"You don't have to go to school today, love," says me Dad.

"What about tomorrow?"

"I don't know."

"When are we coming back?"

Me Mam looks out of the window and me Dad just nods to the taxi man. The taxi starts moving off, slowly down our street, then quicker as we turn on to the main road.

Mam and Dad are both staring out of the window. I look out as well to see what they're looking at, but there's nothing much to see: it's too dark and there's no people, and all the shops are closed. It's not even morning yet and we're going to New Brighton. We've got loads of stuff with us as well. We must be going to stay there. Maybe it's a holiday, that would be great, all three of us, no Auntie Mo to start trouble, just us, together like a proper family.

It's not so dark when the taxi stops cos the sky is lovely and red. We're at the Pier Head. Dad gives the taxi man some money and we get out. We start walking towards the New Brighton Ferry. Dad waves to the taxi man and he drives away. Dad watches the taxi till it's gone round the corner, then he turns round and so do we. We start walking the other way.

"The ferry is that way Dad. We're going the wrong way!"

"Be quiet, we're going this way," says me Dad.

We have to walk for ages and ages and Mam and Dad are all wobbly cos they've got so many bags to carry. I've only got to carry Dottie. We get past this big crane thing and then me Mam stops and puts her bags down. She puts them on top of a dirty old crisp packet and she doesn't even notice.

"We can't stop love, come on," says me Dad.

"Brian, me arms are knackered," she says and then she shakes her arms up and down.

"I know love, but we've got to keep moving." Dad grabs two of the bags she's carrying and starts walking again. He's got so many bags he's a bit like the horse in the Western film. I wish I had me horse. Sparkle could carry all the bags for us and give us a lift as well. Me Mam looks really tired and I can hear her huffing and puffing.

We walk for ages until we get to a place with big glass windows. Behind it is a big boat. A gigantic boat. The one that goes to Ireland. Dad makes us stand still and mind the bags while he goes up to the ticket place. I can see him rooting in all his pockets for money. Dad's got loads of pockets, inside his coat and outside, in his trousers as well. He calls me Mam. She goes over to him and roots in her bag for her purse, then she takes out some coins and gives them to the ticket man.

We go along a corridor to another room. There's two men in the room, they look like coppers only they've got no helmets. They've got a really tall desk each to stand behind. Dad bends down to me and whispers in me ear, "Keep your mouth shut whatever you do. Don't say a thing."

"What is the purpose of your trip, Sir?" says one of the men.

"Holiday," says me Dad.

"How long are you staying?"

"A couple of weeks."

"And what will you be doing over there?"

"Visiting family and just having a break, you know."

"I don't know, Sir, that's why I'm asking you. Now, have you been to Ireland before?"

"Yeah."

"How many times?"

"Two or three."

The man looks at the other man and he makes his eyes all squinty.

"And what was the purpose of those trips?"

"Same thing, just for a break."

"Is this your wife and daughter, Sir?"

"Yeah."

The man peers at me.

"How old are you, little girl?"

I don't answer.

"Too young to play with matches anyway, wouldn't you think, Sir?" he says, looking at me Dad and putting his eyebrows up.

I open the matchbox and pull Dottie out.

"It's not matches, it's a doll's bed," I say, cos I forget I'm not allowed to speak. I think I'm gonna get smacked for talking. I don't. Dad just smiles and pats me on the head.

"That's a nice doll. What's her name then?" asks the man.

This time I remember not to say anything.

"That's a quiet one, isn't she?"

"She's a bit shy," says me Mam.

"OK. Right you can go on. Have a nice trip and be careful over there, it's a dangerous place you know."

"Not where we're going," says me Dad.

"Whatever you say," says the man. The other man looks at us and shakes his head.

We have to walk across this big long thing, like a corridor with windows, only it's really high up. It goes from the big building to the door of the boat. There's two men standing by the door and they point at a room. There's loads of people putting bags in and Dad puts ours in as well. Inside the boat is loads of corridors and stairs. We go up the stairs to the deck. Mam and Dad sit down on a bench and I sit beside them.

"Why are we going to Ireland? Is it cos of the copper and Piggy . . ."

"Shush, we're never going to talk about that again, never, do you understand? This is a new start for all of us. We're going to forget all that . . . stuff. From now on everything's going to be different. You're going to be good . . . we're all going to be good."

I look at me Mam and she nods. I nod back cos this time I know I'm going to be good. It'll be easy when there's miles and miles of sea between us and Piggy Monk Square and it's way too far for Auntie Mo to come and visit.

I go to the side of the boat and look down. The water looks all green and dirty. There's nasty yellow foam and lots of tyres and bits of rubbish floating in it. Then the horn goes off. It's really loud and everyone puts their hands over their ears. Me Dad puts his arm around me Mam and she puts her head on his shoulder. I run back and sit beside me Dad. He puts his arm around me too. The boat starts moving and all of a sudden there's loads of seagulls flying above our heads. They make squawky noises and they start to follow the boat. The boat goes really fast and makes huge splashes, and big white waves that spread across the water, much bigger than the waves from the New Brighton Ferry. Little drops splash on our faces, but we don't go downstairs. We stay sitting on our bench on the deck, getting wet and watching the seagulls. One by one they stop following the boat until there's only three left. It's the same three seagulls that followed me and Josie to New Brighton. I know, cos the biggest one of them has got a black mark on its underneath. There's three of us and three of them. They're going to be our special seagulls. They keep following us. Mam and Dad are looking up at them as well. Mam twists her wedding ring round and round. Dad takes her hand. I think the seagulls are going to follow us all the way. I think they're going to bring us luck.

Also available in ISIS Large Print:

His Coldest Winter

Derek Beaven

One of our most uncompromisingly individual and undervalued novelists. **Guardian**

An unabashed celebration of ordinary England in its last moments of technological supremacy. **Telegraph**

On Boxing Day 1962 it began to snow. Over the next two months England froze. It was the coldest winter since 1740. The sea iced over. Cars could be driven across the Thames.

Riding home from London in that first snowfall, on the powerful motorbike he was given for Christmas, 17-year-old Alan Rae has a brush with death. Immediately he meets a girl, Cynthia, who will change his life. But someone else is equally preoccupied with her: Geoffrey, a young scientist who works with Alan's father in the race with the Americans and the Russians to develop the microchip. Alan, Geoffrey and Cynthia become linked by a web of secrets which, while the country remains in icy suspension, threatens everything they ever trusted.

ISBN 0-7531-7461-8 **(hb)**
ISBN 0-7531-7462-6 **(pb)**

Eleanor Rigby

Douglas Coupland

A powerful and moving examination of a life lived negotiating loneliness.   **Independent**

Skilful plotting and appealing characters.   **Telegraph**

Funny, unexpected and fragile.   **Guardian**

Liz Dunn is 42 years old, and lonely. Her house is like "a spinster's cell block", and she may or may not snore — there's never been anybody to tell her. Then one day in 1997, with the comet Hale Bopp burning bright in the blue-black sky, Liz receives an urgent phone call asking her to visit a young man in hospital. All at once, the loneliness that has come to define her is ripped away by this funny, smart, handsome young stranger, Jeremy. Her son.

ISBN 0-7531-7375-1 (hb)
ISBN 0-7531-7376-X (pb)